FOOL'S GOLD

GW00802422

Recent Titles by Vivien Armstrong

CLOSE CALL *
DEAD IN THE WATER*
FOOL'S GOLD*
THE HONEY TRAP
SLEIGHT OF HAND
THE WRONG ROAD *

* *available from Severn House*

FOOL'S GOLD

Vivien Armstrong

This first world edition published in Great Britain 2000 by
SEVERN HOUSE PUBLISHERS LTD of
9–15 High Street, Sutton, Surrey SM1 1DF.
This first world edition published in the U.S.A. 2000 by
SEVERN HOUSE PUBLISHERS INC of
595 Madison Avenue, New York, N.Y. 10022.

British Library Cataloguing in Publication Data

Armstrong,   Vivien
    Fool's gold
    1.Detective and mystery stories
    I. Title
    823.9'14 [F]

    ISBN 0-7278-5531-X

Typeset by Palimpsest Book Production Ltd.
Polmont, Stirlingshire, Scotland.
Printed and bound in Great Britain by
MPG Books Ltd, Bodmin, Cornwall.

One

I t was the sudden burst of light from the landing which woke her. A child in pyjamas stood silhouetted in the doorway, his hair a bright halo against the glare of the dangling lightbulb. She raised her head: a bad move. Little hammers started up behind her eyes.

"Who are you?" he said.

The sleeping log of the man beside her wasn't going to answer.

"Anabel," she croaked.

The boy moved to the bed clutching a threadbare teddy, its body limp from affection. He nodded and climbed over to snuggle between them, sucking his thumb, the toy's fur harsh against her bare flesh. She lay rigid, disorientated, mind racing. Where the hell was she? And how did she come to be in bed with this child in a house with a man seemingly a stranger? Aware that closing her eyes would set her head churning again she breathed deeply, hoping this was all some sort of nightmare.

'Who are you?' the boy had said. The real question was: who were *they*? And where in God's name was this?

The man stirred, cradling the boy in his sleep, the light streaming from the open door throwing his profile into focus. Solomon Cheyney. The brainbox jangled into life at last. The

1

private view. At Cheyney's gallery. Anabel shivered, alive to the realisation that she had absolutely no recollection of how she got here. The child's unblinking gaze followed her around the room as she silently gathered up her clothes and slipped away.

Two

Her appointment with the Art Editor that morning was scheduled for ten. Freshly showered, hair shining, and her portfolio under her arm, Anabel Gordon had regained her composure – the shock of finding herself shacked up with what amounted to a virtual stranger was now no more than a wagging finger at the back of her mind, just one more spiral on this accelerating vortex she seemed to be sucked into.

Her dealings with Abigail Griffith were long-standing, their camaraderie taking on a slipshod warmth, a rare commodity in the media business and especially so in the offices of *Eve Now* magazine, the token cultural input for ladies who lunch. There were few enough slots for any type of art illustration, trendy graphics being the thing, but any opportunity which arose Gail put Anabel's way. She sat at her desk enveloped in a pall of cigarette smoke, her curranty eyes missing nothing, especially not the heavy circles under Annie Gordon's eyes and the paper-white skin almost transparent in its fragility.

They laid her drawings across the desk, Gail's thick fingers turning the sheets with delicacy, Anabel stabbing at the details and urgently stressing her motif. The colour-washed sketches were of botanical exactitude but elegantly sprawled across each sheet with a light touch, just right for the Health Shock spring edition.

"Excellent."

"Thanks, Gail. Any hope of an advance? I'm totally skint. Got my phone cut off last week, would you believe?"

"Out of my hands, sweetie. What's the problem? Run out of commissions? You're still doing those copycat jobs, aren't you?"

"Van Gogh for less than £200? Famous master works – sunflowers by the yard, woman with big boobs having a Rubensesque paddle? Yeah!" Anabel's laugh was bitter as lemons. She sobered, reaching across the desk to help herself to one of Gail's cigarettes. "Actually, I've just finished something for a regular client, a retired dealer living in Italy. I'm flying out with it on Friday morning. He's asked me to stay on for a month and do some sketches of his villa. Almost a holiday . . ."

Gail's big laugh cantered round the room: no wonder her nickname in the outer offices was Gee-Gee. "You watch it, you'll wake up one morning in bed with the old bugger."

Anabel winced.

"Seriously, love. Sketches of the villa! Give me a break. You're too old for that old foreplay, Annie. He is paying air fare and expenses, I presume?"

"Sure. Only I need something decent to wear in the evenings – Philip's still very influential with the European auction houses, verifies paintings and so on – a terrific networker! Last time I was over he took me to a party in Milan but my Oxfam retro just wasn't up to the competition. It could be just the intro I need, Gail. Could lead on to some really worthwhile commissions."

"Copying?"

"No!" Her temper flared. "That's just to pay the rent. Original work. I'm thirty-six years old for Christ's sake. And barely dipped my toe in the market so far."

4

"Getting desperate?"

"You bet. So desperate I got pissed at a private view last night and woke up this morning with a classic headbanger and in bed with a guy I barely recognised. Haven't done that since the heady days when I was at art college! Seriously, Gail, I could go right off men!" She grimaced and in an effort to diffuse the whingeing tone, no way to impress Abigail Griffith, added, "Actually there were three of us."

"Two *men*?"

She laughed. "Sort of. This little boy jumped in between us, calm as you like. Obviously seen it all before. I'd no idea Solomon Cheyney had kids, did you?"

"The gallery owner?" Gail shrugged and the talk was channelled to more cheerful topics before she tossed an invitation across the desk.

"Designer sale. Zelini's. No use to me, Annie. You take it. *Very* exclusive threads."

Anabel reached for the card, an impressive stiffy for an invitation-only evening sale at a private address in a street behind Chelsea Green.

"It's tonight, Gail. Anyway, I can't afford her stuff – it's way out of my league."

"Bollocks! End of season. Zelini practically gives it away, but on the quiet – doesn't want the riff-raff to muscle in and make a bunfight of it. I took a peek last season but it's more your style. Put it on your plastic. Look at it as an investment, Annie. Bait for those big time punters you'll be angling for in Italy."

Anabel fingered the engraved card and decided to give it a look-over at least. No harm in looking. Gee-Gee was right. Bait.

*　　*　　*

The house where the Zelini sale was being held was part of a stuccoed terrace west of Pond Place, well away from the Belgravia showroom and discreetly anonymous. Anabel rang the bell, wondering if, after all, this was such a good idea. When a butler in full fig opened the door she knew she was out of her depth and when he ushered her in, took Abigail Griffith's invitation card and motioned her to sign the visitors' book on the hall table, she was sure of it.

The collection was being shown on the first floor and as she mounted the stairs a murmur of voices filtered through closed doors. The first room off the landing contained nothing but evening wraps and hand-embroidered cloaks, all very Phantom of the Opera but hardly investment material. A second door opened on to a drawing room cleared of furniture and pitilessly top-lit, the walls obscured by clothes rails and two full-length mirrors. An anteroom leading off from this was being used as a dressing area, overseen by a viper in a tubular jersey dress.

Anabel was one of the last customers, it would seem – the rails plundered, a worried-looking man at a table in the corner anxiously totting up the sales slips and eyeing the dwindling clientele. Actually, Gail was right: prices were slashed, probably due to the fact that the remaining model sizes limited sales to anorexic teenagers. She hit on a promising midnight blue confection with crystal embroidered straps, and an absolutely stunning little number in black crepe.

The changing room was a windowless boxroom casually divided by linen screens, the air thick with cigarette smoke. Customers jammed themselves into the cubicles or changed in full view, the usual crowd of fashion victims, a bit shop-soiled themselves. She found herself sharing a corner with a Twiggy lookalike who shimmied into a beaded slip, no more than a wisp of raw silk. Anabel dumped her crumpled suit on the floor and after a swift try-on and an encouraging nod from Twiggy, plumped for the black.

Suddenly the lights went out. A fire alarm shrilled through the building. The cashier burst in and shouted at them all to leave, the basement already alight, he bawled, but if they were quick . . . Screams rent the house and in the total blackness scrambling about on the carpet for her discarded suit proved impossible. Anabel found herself shoved aside, sprawling under the stilettos stampeding for the exit. Frantic efforts to escape took on Titanic proportions, fuelled by the undeniable stench of burning fabric.

Anabel felt about for her handbag and crawled through choking fumes billowing from the stairwell. Losing all sense of direction she panicked, couldn't locate the stairs and found herself in the second sales room knowing she had only minutes before being overcome by the smoke. She fell against a table, eyes streaming, and the display overturned, shrouding her in one of the velvet capes. Blinded by smoke she slung her bag round her neck and groped her way along the wall, wrapping herself in the voluminous folds before hurling a chair at the window. The glass shattered and she climbed over the sill, barely registering the pain as a shard ripped through the black crepe dress to slash her thigh before she crashed into a shrubbery below. A dense privet bush had broken her fall and, winded, she scrambled to her feet.

Opening one streaming eye Anabel found herself alone in the back garden, the shrieks and clatter of the disaster focussed on the front street where two fire engines screamed to a halt, lights blazing, sirens adding to the decibels. She limped to the fence and climbed over a trellis into a cul-de-sac crowded with onlookers gazing up at the flames and smoke now belching from the upper windows.

Cocooned in the all-enveloping cape Anabel slid unnoticed through the crowd of gibbering onlookers and, shoeless, shuffled to the Green. A taxi idled, the driver mesmerised by the inferno, astonished to find himself with a fare clambering aboard like a shipwrecked survivor and coughing her lungs out. At last she managed to gasp out her address, the overwhelming desire to be as far away as possible driving out all thoughts but her near death experience. Even the cabdriver realised his fare was in no fit state for small talk.

Home. Scrabbling at the bottom of her bag she found a loose tenner she must have forgotten about but no keys. She dragged herself out on to the pavement, now gripped with uncontrollable tremors, still coughing like a chain smoker and longing only to wrap herself round a huge slug of whisky. She resorted to the spare key hidden in the windowbox for emergencies and, safe inside, threw herself on the bed and passed out.

It was much later that she discovered that the handbag so tenaciously clung to throughout the disaster was not hers at all. It looked exactly like her own, certainly: same textured leather, same little gilt padlock and double straps, the Paris maker's name discreetly embossed inside. But it was not the bag she had started out with. This one was your actual crocodile.

Anabel's had been a knock-off from Hong Kong, a cheap copy with all the right touches including its own cotton storage bag – but intrinsically false. This bag was the real McCoy, reeking of money, an item retailing at squillions of francs, an accessory toted only by the starriest of rich bitches.

In the frantic scramble to get out of Zelini's firehouse Anabel had grabbed the Twiggy girl's authentic item. Bloody hell . . .

Three

"Hi! My name's Annie Gordon. I was at Zelini's last night – we shared a cubicle. The girl with the black dress?"

"Oh – er . . . yes, sure. I got shoved out by that saleswoman. You OK?"

"I'm fine. Just a cut leg. Problem is I picked up your handbag by mistake. It's just like mine and in the dark and all that smoke—"

"My bag? You sure? I thought it was torched!" The voice was ragged with tension, the vowels raw as only a bred-in-the-bone Neasden girl's could be.

"Sorry. I should have telephoned last night, you must have been worried sick. I'll bring it over, shall I? On my way to work."

"Look." The Twiggy girl's tone dropped to a barely audible whisper. "Can you meet me at Turner House? It's a new development on the South Bank – not far from the Oxo tower. The show flat on the top floor? Ten o'clock."

Anabel stiffened. "Well, I do realise it was my mistake but the South Bank's well off my beat actually. Couldn't we meet somewhere more central? I couldn't find your address in your organiser – just the mobile phone bill – but how about if I put the bag in a taxi and send it over and—?"

She cut in. "I can't talk now. But I really *need* my stuff,

9

Abby. Right away, and I can't have it going missing again. Be a duck. Get a cab, I'll pay and they'll be a big reward when you get here. Honest!" The pleading grew urgent. Desperate, Anabel conceded, as only one who had lost and found all her most personal items within twenty-four hours could be.

Reluctantly, she agreed, jotting down the directions on the back of one of Dimitri's menu cards. It was only when she had rung off that she realised she hadn't asked the girl's name.

Since her phone had been cut off Anabel had taken to using the pay phone in the cafe downstairs, a greasy spoon run by a hairy Greek called Georghiou. Anabel and Dimitri were mates, his 'full English breakfast' substituting a wodge of missed meals when her budget ran low.

The cafe, optimistically called the Adelphi Grill, occupied the corner of a row of shops at the back end of Brixton market. Anabel's flat above the caff boasted its own entrance off the street, a north light and a panoramic view of chimneypots which she kidded herself could, on a wet day, double for Montmartre. The downside was an ever-present stench of rancid cooking oil that hung about the stairwell like a spectre.

She sidled out of the booth and sat up at the counter with an espresso strong enough to tar a road. Dimitri's coffee was special and the hubbub of market traders jammed at the plastic topped tables, scoffing bacon butties before the real day's work set in, seemed a suitable backdrop for her black mood. She gazed at her reflection in the pitted glass backing Dimitri's counter: a bush of black curly hair flaring round pallid features staring back at her with the eyes of a stranger. Even allowing for the bleak reportage Dimitri's mirror afforded, Anabel knew that time was running out. Her work was shit. The men in her life were shit. And when the vague promise of a reward from a woman whose handbag she had stolen was propelling her to tack across London in the hope of picking up a few quid, the water in the well was indeed bitter.

She checked the time. Eight fifteen. Waving cheerily to Dimitri, Anabel climbed back up to her garret, determined to look on the bright side. After all there was her free flight to Pisa in the morning and the prospect of April in Tuscany. Even in the company of old Philip Barclayson the break would be paradise: the chance to get some real work done and three meals a day thrown in.

She was just starting to pack up her version of Whistler's portrait of Cicely Alexander ready for the journey when the doorbell shrilled with the determination of a drugs bust. She propped the unframed copy against the wall and ran downstairs to open the door.

Abigail Griffith stood on the step, peroxide hair all anyhow, four-square figure implacable.

"Thank Christ you're here," she burst out, pushing past and up the stairs. Anabel fizzed with the possible permutations for this unprecedented visitation. The big woman threw herself on the sofa and, sloshing down the dregs left over from Anabel's anaesthesia the night before, closed her eyes. Her skin appeared unhealthily mottled, stripped of its normal professional patina. Anabel stood in the doorway, waiting for a clue.

Gail finally surfaced, glanced at her watch and, fixing the little black eyes venomously on her quarry, blurted out, "My car's on a yellow line. Hell, Annie, I don't need this first thing."

"What?"

"Bloody police crashing in on me before I'm even out of the pit, wanting to know if I'm dead or alive."

"Dead?"

"Stop gawping. You look like a goldfish."

"Gail, I've no idea what you're on about. Wait, I'll make some coffee."

Abigail followed her into the kitchen, finally coming down off her high horse as the caffeine hit the button.

"A Sergeant Culley. Checking up on me. Thought I was some fucking corpse they'd found at Zelini's after the fire."

"But you weren't even there!"

"Of course I wasn't. But apparently he had some sort of list and my name was on it. You didn't go either, of course. But it didn't dawn on me till I'd thrown him out that you *might* have been there. Within twenty seconds I pictured you fried in that place. And all my fault! I jammed on a jacket and bombed over here, praying like a born-again. Didn't even put on my mascara." This last thrust failed to hold back the tears brimming under reddened eyelids. Gail pitched forward, clasping the girl in a trembling embrace, the shock, Anabel concluded, reaching parts of that streetwise editor's heart no-one had dreamed of.

"Oh, Gail. I'm *so* sorry. And you really thought I was the corpse? You drove straight over?"

The puffy eyes hardened. "Only because your phone's cut off, you cow. Have you no idea of the fuss? The papers are full of it this morning. Quote. 'Fire Blazes Designer Sale. Unidentified Body Found in Lavatory. Two still in intensive care and customers – including Marisa Frankel, the movie star – suffering from smoke inhalation.' Unquote."

"Oh my."

"And *you*, my dark angel, were not even on the premises!" Gail started to laugh, shaking in a paroxysm of near hysteria. It suddenly occurred to Anabel that Gee-Gee's affection ran on lines she had never suspected. She stepped back, facing Gail across the kitchen table.

"Actually, I was there. I got out at the back. Wait, I'll show you."

Anabel hurried into the living room and recovered the torn Zelini cocktail dress from the waste bin.

"Look. I climbed out the window, slicing up my leg on the glass en route, and fell into the garden. Then I legged it like a bat out of hell. Sheer terror. I've never been within a hundred miles of a house fire before, the speed the flames take hold is truly horrific. It never occurred to me that the police would be bothering you. I haven't really had time to think . . ."

Gail fingered the black crepe, fixing Anabel in jaundiced appraisal.

"You escaped the fire in *this*?"

"Believe me, there was no time to return the goods."

"You'd already paid for this rag?"

"No, of course not. I was trying it on when the alarm went off. The lights went out. Smoke everywhere. I lost my suit, my shoes – even my bag," she added. "And I'm off to Italy first thing tomorrow."

"Poor baby. Here, leave this with me." She shoved the dress in her tote bag. "I'll get the office lawyer on to it. Make an insurance claim. After all you were representing the magazine, were you not? A suit and shoes and a handbag. Seven hundred at least and that's without the personal injury. Might even need plastic surgery, never know. Make a full statement and send it over by bike messenger before noon. And send me your address when you get to Italy. A month you said? And you'd better get to a quack before the cuts start to heal." She scrabbled in her bag and jotted down an address on the back of her business card. "Here, this bloke's on the payroll, tell him it's an emergency and he's to send the bill to the office. Get him to sign a chitty for the insurance claim and fax it to me with photographs if possible. And, on second thoughts, you'd better sign in with Sergeant Culley at the Chelsea nick so he can cross you off his obituary list."

"Is all this really necessary? I really haven't time to fit everything in – I've got to pack up for tomorrow and get to the bank. I haven't cancelled my credit cards yet. Getting bogged down with a police enquiry is the last thing I need; it's not even as if I could tell them anything."

Gail's raised eyebrow said it all. Gathering up her bag and keys she made for the door, turning to examine the tiny apartment for the first time.

"This really is a grotty hole, Annie. If you decide to share with me you'd find Hampstead's much healthier than Brixton or we could rent a proper studio for you."

Leaving Anabel with a maelstrom of confusing options, she stomped down the stairs just in time to collar a traffic warden sizing up her red MG.

Anabel fell on to the sofa, poleaxed by the turn of events, unsure what she had let herself in for with Abigail Griffith, so far regarded merely as a staunch friend and useful contact. Well, what do you know? There has to be a first time for everything but seeing Gail in this new light certainly made a difference. She shrugged off this little black cloud and threw her energies into correcting the frayed image she had glimpsed in Dimitri's mirror to something which her anonymous Twiggy friend would recognise as the girl from Zelini's.

She stock-checked the contents of the magnificent crocodile handbag. The usual stuff: make-up, keys, perfume, a gold lighter and a half pack of cigarettes, a passport in the name of Kimberley Ada Carter with the usual nervy photo-booth shot of the Twiggy lookalike. The biggest item, a bulging organiser chock-a-block with addresses, pages of figures and cryptic references, had been wrapped in a Hermes silk square. She put these things back as she had found them, anxious not to seem nosy. But the contents of this stranger's bag were too tempting. She sifted the rest of the stuff in her lap: loose change and a bundle of fifties in a black purse were no surprise but, hey-ho, what have we here? A wallet crammed with hundred dollar bills. A bloody fortune. Only thing was the wallet also contained a second passport. A friend? No way. Same girl, same heart-shaped birthmark perched at the corner of the lips, same date of birth. But this blonde was Swiss and her name allegedly Martha Ferrero.

Four

Anabel taped up the jagged cut on her thigh with half a dozen plasters, the only items in her first aid box apart from a dusty packet of aspirins. Gail was right. She ought to get a doctor to look it over, the gash still oozing blood and flaring dangerously. She winced. As if there wasn't enough to do. And if this Twiggy creature with her two passports had not promised a hefty reward for the return of her handbag, this unwanted jaunt would have featured well down her list. Still, if Twiggy *was* paying for the taxi a little detour wouldn't hurt anyone.

It was almost ten before she set off – taming her unruly cloud of curly hair and buffing her alabaster complexion to a more healthy glow took more time than she bargained for. The ultimate effect, set off with a sapphire wool miniskirt and black suede thigh boots would do the trick, especially as first stop was the bank. Anabel stowed the crocodile bag in a plastic carrier and ran downstairs, slamming the door in a frisson of impatience.

She told the cab driver to wait and breezed in to claim her favourite under-manager, a blushing young man seated behind his splendid desk in the so-called customer-friendly banking hall. Listening to her dilemma, the lost handbag and credit cards, Anabel's target crumpled under her charm assault

16

and went away to fetch her Italian cash for the journey plus traveller's cheques.

Outside, she breathed the fresh morning breeze with an air of triumph, jolted the taxi driver from Page Three and urged him to put his foot down. Next stop: the show flat at Turner House.

The journey took some time, the rush hour jams now seemingly extended to all-day gridlock. Turner House proved to be a recently completed tower block overlooking the river, the lower floors allocated to a shopping centre of the restaurant-cum-sports-gear variety, a Curzon Street hairdressers already going great guns in their new Turner House branch in the atrium.

Anabel got a receipt from the cabbie and trotted through to reception where they handed her a brochure which she skimmed in the lift taking her up to the penthouse suite. Turner House was certainly a far cry from her Brixton pad, boasting a leisure complex, underground car park and a fully operational IT business centre, whatever that was.

The lift soundlessly decanted her at the open door of the show flat and a nice young Jeremy type in a double-breasted suit and tasselled loafers surged towards her, all teeth and professional laughter lines. Anabel wafted her brochure in a dismissive gesture and stalked inside, a ready apology on her lips for poor Twiggy who had presumably been cooling her heels here for nearly an hour. In fact, the girl was nowhere to be seen and in Anabel's swift recce of the penthouse it became increasingly obvious that Twiggy's anxiety to retrieve her missing property was on a strict time limit.

The salesman zoomed in as she emerged from the state-of-the-art television room but before he could launch into his pitch Anabel explained her mission.

"My friend was to meet me here – Kimberley?"

The estate-agent clone visibly deflated, the smile doused like a rat in a sewer. Anabel felt a twinge of pity – offloading million-dollar flats in these recessionary times must be hard graft.

"Why didn't you say?" he pouted. "It's her day off."

"She works here?"

"Works?" he snorted. "I suppose you could call it that. She shags the boss, Raymond Turner, and he lets her pat cushions here and calls her the Design Consultant."

Nonplussed, Anabel put on her knowing look. "Ah, *that* Raymond Turner. What else does she do?"

"Actually, she's not that bad," he conceded. "Kim does the flowers and changes the room layouts from time to time. Drops in most days to check things over. I thought you said she was a friend of yours?"

"We only met once. I need to speak to her about something she left at a party last night."

"She'll be in later. Why don't you wait? Can I get you a coffee? Some tea?" The Jeremy had relaxed since he discovered this tasty morsel with the bundle of black curly hair did not have to be wooed like a real client, and, with more time to spare, Anabel considered a tête-à-tête on a sofa overlooking the Thames wouldn't go amiss either. But, Sod's law, there was no time to dally with the guy even for a coffee break.

"Look, I'm really pushed, Mr . . . er . . . ?"

"Bailey. Andy Bailey."

"Can I leave Kim a note? I'll call back later this afternoon. A rain check on that coffee maybe?"

"No problem. I'll fax it straight over to her at Head Office."

She scribbled on the back of her brochure, irritated by the sheer bloody inconvenience of chasing up this bimbo, Kimberley Carter.

"May I use your phone, Andy? I need a doctor."

His eyes widened but, like a well-trained retriever, he handed over his mobile and she gave him the note before punching in the number of the doctor Gail had insisted she consult about the 'personal injury' suffered in the course of her escape from the Zelini fire. Andy Bailey scanned the note on the brochure as the girl with the big brown eyes made her appointment in Harley Street.

'Kimberley. Sorry I missed you,' he read. 'Your handbag's safe with A.G. but we need to meet before tomorrow. I'll call back later today, so have what we agreed ready as we can't waste any more time and I need the money.'

She handed back his phone and grinned.

"Thanks, Andy. See you later." He visibly brightened and showed her to the lift.

As she left the building it occurred to her why the name Turner Developments had rung a bell. It had been the name on the phone bill she had found crushed at the bottom of Kim's bag. Totting up her expenses so far and reckoning the time it would take to cross London to the doctor's surgery in time for her urgent appointment, Anabel decided Kimberley's no-show would cost her. She would just have to dip into the girl's bulging wallet yet again and bill her for a second taxi ride, so there. As she relaxed in the cab, cursing the 'No Smoking Please' sign pointedly displayed on the driver's partition, another interesting thought surfaced. For all the hand-tooled leather and gold knick-knacks, Kimberley Carter's bag contained no credit cards. Odd. Maybe with Raymond Turner as a sugar daddy, cash was never a problem. And they always said, 'blondes have more fun'.

By the time she left the doctor's surgery all strapped up and photographed from every angle, it was well past one, the lunch hour being no time to find Gee-Gee Griffith trapped behind her desk at *Eve Now*. Anyway after such a lousy morning her own insides were growling for sustenance. She hailed another cab. This could become a habit with a crocodile purse crammed with lolly at her disposal but time was pressing and there were all those other little errands to attend to – crating up the picture for a start. With a jolt Anabel suddenly remembered Gail's insistence that she checked in with Sergeant Culley at the Chelsea nick. Hell fire!

"Well, you'll just have to get in the queue, Sergeant," she muttered as she fitted her key in the lock.

What happened to the rest of the day Anabel tried not to think about. Boxing up poor little 'Cicely Alexander' for the flight was a job and a half and typing up a report for Gee-Gee's lawyer and faxing it to the magazine offices took even longer. Sorting out her own depleted wardrobe for Italy was on a par with sharing out the loaves and fishes. In desperation she shoved the velvet opera cloak in her suitcase, horribly aware that this expensive acquisition from the Zelini sale had entirely slipped her mind when recounting her adventures to Gail Griffith that morning.

But it had to be admitted the big bite out of the schedule was what she always tried to shy away from: the time it took to be with Ronnie. Taking the tube to Kings Cross was supposed to beat the traffic but there was some sort of go-slow or breakdown which left Anabel trapped in a dark tunnel with hundreds of fuming commuters. The lift at Ronnie's tower block was, as ever, out of service and lugging her bag of groceries up the concrete stairs left her aching with the sheer brutality of life in general. Ronnie was in a bad mood, violent and abusive, but, even so, it was never easy to tear herself away, and admitting that work would take her abroad for at least a month was greeted with undisguised rancour. Escaping the rancid set of rooms with both relief and heartfelt reluctance was a burden she must learn to live with. Because loving Ronnie gave her life its only joy.

Back home, she did, however, diligently parcel up the torn cocktail dress and mail it to the lawyer's office with a covering note assuring him the doctor had promised to send him directly a professional opinion on her cuts together with the photographs as soon as they were processed. But registering her survival with Detective Sergeant Culley would just have to go hang. Surely they had, by now, identified the corpse found at the scene of the Zelini fire? Clocking in with the fuzz tonight might even prevent her flight to Pisa next morning, knowing the red tape knotting up any sort of police investigation.

When she at last got round to phoning the show flat at Turner House Andy had already locked up and gone home and she was reduced to leaving a terse message for Kimberley Carter on the answer machine. She deliberately did not leave her name or her contact number care of Dimitri's caff downstairs, insisting the girl met her at the check-in desk at the airport before her flight to Pisa next morning. She was fed up with chasing round like some sort of fairy godmother. Kim knew very well who had her poxy bag and her insistence that its return was of the utmost urgency cut no ice when the cow had not even bothered to turn up at the penthouse that morning. Luckily, there had been ample cash available to pay for the taxis but what about that promised reward?

Anabel felt her temper rising as she rushed about her squalid flat thinking about the easy-come-easy-go attitude of Mr Turner Development's Girl Friday. She would ring her from the airport in the morning if she didn't show up and suggest sending the bloody handbag to Turner Developments

Head Office and let Kimberley-sodding-Carter talk her way out of those embarrassing twin passports with her boss.

To be fair, she *could* have left the bag with Andy Bailey but human nature being what it was, who could blame the man for sifting through Kimberley's stuff himself? And with all those dollar bills and the cache of sterling who would believe a penniless art copyist if the money went walkabout? That's the trouble with me, Anabel decided. I just assume that every good-looking guy who gets in my sights is a double-crossing fink. It was becoming second nature, goddammit.

Five

Detective Sergeant Culley stood in the rain outside Anna Zelini's private house waiting for the butler to open up. The place looked uncared for, the spring bulbs flowering in the border each side of a path clotted with weeds, the windows fronting the street shuttered, no lights or signs of occupation glimmering out on to the heavy evening traffic as it made slow progress towards Knightsbridge.

Tom Culley rang the bell again, feeling the wet penetrate his suede shoes like blotting paper. Eventually bolts were dragged back and the door swung open, the butler, dressed in a black jacket and striped trousers, glowering at the unexpected caller.

"Mr Wiffin?"

The man was startled, the ready phrases about his employer's absence drying on his lips. He looked as unkempt as the ragged garden, a day's stubble darkening his jowls, two missing buttons from his waistcoat leaving a frill of shirt frothing over the top of his trousers.

Culley flashed his ID and after careful scrutiny Wiffin allowed him inside. The young policeman shook out his wet raincoat and threw it on a carved oak chair standing against the wall. The vestibule of the regency house was dimly lit, the checkerboard marble floor glowing in the twilight afforded by a chandelier short of several candle bulbs.

Wiffin stood firm and, only after a further exchange regarding the purpose of the police visit, reluctantly led Culley down to the basement where a back room fairly rocked with heat from an electric fire, the TV transmitting the busty delights of a starspangled game show. It was, Culley supposed, a sort of snuggery, and from the number of bottles on the sideboard and the plate of half-eaten ham rolls by his leather armchair the butler did not go short of home comforts.

Wiffin got back to his supper, clamping on his wad with the click and slurp of badly fitting dentures. Culley's stomach growled – the Inspector, in his anxiety to wrap up the Zelini case, had buried the duty rotas to the background music of a whimpering chorus of complaint. Culley switched off the television and seated himself at the table, placing his notebook and the Zelini visitors' book before him. The ledger the sales customers had been obliged to sign on arrival was little damaged, only a few black smuts and scorch marks evidence of its recovery from the fire. Culley decided to try and smooth-talk the butler through what promised to be a tricky interview.

"Saving the visitors' book is a credit to you, sir. It is, of course, invaluable to our investigation."

"No-one's identified the corpse then?"

"No. That's the trouble, Mr Wiffin. Are you absolutely certain no lady came through the door without signing the book?"

Wiffin drew himself up, his colour rising.

"I told your Inspector all this last night. No-one crossed the bloody threshold without me checking the invite and making them sign in. How many more times do I have to tell you people?"

Culley raised his hand in mute apology and watched Wiffin down a double vodka before going on.

"There is no criticism of your efficiency, Mr Wiffin. On the contrary. But you can see our problem, can't you? May we please go over the names once again?"

Wiffin sighed and moved to a chair next to Culley at the table, the overhead light casting a feeble glow over the papers spread across the cloth. The visitors' book took centre stage and those few charred invitation cards which had been salvaged fanned out like curling autumn leaves. Culley quoted from a typewritten list, ticking off each name against the signatures in the visitors' book which Wiffin confirmed.

"Look, I'm sorry to bother you with all this yet again, sir, but we do find a few discrepancies." Baulking Wiffin's protest, Culley pressed on. "Now, these are the ones which raise some problems. All these ladies we have ticked off are hospitalised or otherwise accounted for. But there are four names which are in the book and not listed on the invitation list provided by Madame Zelini's secretary and there are another two whose signatures appear in the visitors' book but who swear they were never there."

"Nothing to do with me, Sergeant. Them girls in the office always snitch a few blanks and pass them on to their mates. You'd be better off putting that toffee-nosed secretary Mrs Aynesly-Foster through the mincer. She knows what goes on behind Madame's back same as me. All I know is the ones what had the invites signed my book like I said. I wasn't issued no typed invitation list to check against the names on the cards."

His bloodshot eye fixed on Culley like the wrath of god.

"You seem to have been particularly careful, Mr Wiffin. It was, after all, only a dress sale, hardly entrance to a bank vault."

"Madame's very fussy about the people what wear her stuff.

Don't want any old scrubbers muscling in. Spoils the image, she says."

"Even so . . ."

Wiffin, clearly a man to take umbrage at any tilt at his efficiency, glared at Culley.

"I was a prison warder for fifteen years before I took up this butlering lark. After counting heads in and out of the exercise yard day in and day out, checking a few women through the front door is second nature."

Culley sighed. "Please bear with me, Mr Wiffin. If I may?" He swivelled the book to face the butler. "If a few invitations went astray or, as you say, the office staff distributed them to friends, why is it that two of these women named in the book and who are listed on the office copy Madame Zelini's secretary passed to the police, insist they were never present?"

"You tell me!"

"Here. There's a Mrs Halley of Chart Street signed the visitors' book but says she wasn't there and a lady called Abigail Griffith of *Eve Now* magazine who insisted to me she also was never on the premises. Any ideas?"

"That Mrs Halley's a liar for a start. I seen her meself. A tall tart with dyed red hair, comes to every Zelini show and buys like Imelda Marcos. Check the till receipts at the sale."

"Unfortunately, the cashier's records went up in flames. Why would this Mrs Halley pretend she wasn't there?"

"Didn't want her old man to find out she was still on the game most likely. Mrs Halley's cheques bounced a couple of times and I was told on the q.t. that 'er 'usband cancelled her credit. Spoke to Madame himself after Christmas. Told her he wouldn't cough up for her debts no more. Shopaholic. Some of these women just can't leave it alone, believe me." As

Wiffin's account gathered enthusiasm the butler's professional delivery shifted down a gear and the former prison officer's took over.

"OK. Well, Mrs Halley's just an example, you might say."

"Checking up on my security methods more like."

Culley stiffened, jotting notes in his file with growing irritation at all this footling paperwork, not to mention the chippiness of his expert witness.

"Well, what about Mrs Griffith?"

"Now that one's definitely a bloody liar. Was the last through the door, remember that one most particular. New customer, never seen her before and most of them at these sales bashes are regulars." He stabbed at the signature, the last in the book and the handwriting clear.

"What did she look like, this Mrs Griffith?"

"It was a Ms. One of them new-fangled titles these feminist people bang on about. Skinny. Had a stack of black frizzy hair like a Hottentot."

Culley relaxed, seeing daylight at last, and, without a hint of triumph, described his own interview with the fourteen-stone art editor.

Wiffin shrugged. "Can't win 'em all. These magazine people got no manners. Madame insists on personal invites only just to keep these swop-shop slags off the premises. Reckon the black-haired girl's the one on the slab then?"

"Could be. *Someone* got in by default."

"And nobody's shouting?"

"No missing person reported so far."

Culley gathered up his papers, stowing the visitors' book in a sealed bag together with the scorched invitation cards.

Wiffin escorted him to the front door, more loquacious since the vodka took the corners off his prickly sensitivities.

"Madame Zelini's abroad you say?" asked Culley.

"Milan. Gets back tomorrow."

"Terrible thing, fire. Gutted that house of hers. Anyone have it in for her, d'you know?"

Wiffin's mouth pursed like a drawstring bag.

"No comment," he muttered, his gaze riveted to the chandelier from which the gossamer threads of a cobweb swung in the feeble glow. "Anyway, the house weren't hers. Rented it from her partner. There's a workroom on the top floor."

Culley shrugged into his mac, nodding at Wiffin as the butler smoothly ejected him on to the rainy street.

He stood under a shop awning and consulted his notebook. It was after nine o'clock. Surely even magazine editors were home from work by now? He phoned Ms Griffith's number and let it ring. The answer machine moved in but he cut the connection: plenty of time to catch up with that one next morning; no need to give her advance warning. The question was, why hadn't she admitted passing over her Zelini invitation when he first interviewed her? Who was Griffith covering for? And if she *was* alive why be shy about coming forward? No evidence of arson had been found though if, as was possible, Zelini's business was not as buoyant as it seemed, the insurance money would come in handy, wouldn't it?

Culley thrust this conjecture aside: the house, according to the butler, was rented from Zelini's business partner – the claim for the loss of the merchandise would not be worth risking an arson investigation, would it? And torching all your regular customers at the same time was hardly commercial. Even so, the fire investigation officers were still sifting through the wreckage. Something would turn up soon.

By eight o'clock next morning Anabel had arranged for her

crated oil painting to be despatched on a later cargo flight and was waiting to book in. Getting to the airport on time had been the usual scramble, her timekeeping chronically flawed, but even the prospect of flying away from the grey skies brooding over the runway could not lift her spirits.

She frowned, trying unsuccessfully to justify her determined getaway. The increasingly nasty anonymous messages left at Turner House for Kimberley Carter remained unanswered and even Gail Griffith had apparently spent the night away from home. A fleeting image of an overweight moggy out on the tiles momentarily lightened her mood but there was still the question of the crocodile handbag, not to mention the police investigation into the Zelini inferno.

Signing Gail's name in the visitors' book had been a knee-jerk reaction to that po-faced butler who was checking the invitations against the signatures and poised to pitch anyone back out in the street like a gatecrasher at a New Year's Eve party. She should have mentioned it to Gee-Gee first off but with her mind cluttered with all those other little guilty secrets it hadn't seemed that important at the time.

Feeling like a shoplifter Anabel slyly re-examined the contents of Kim's bag hidden inside her hand luggage. It certainly was one hell of a hot potato. In a moment of panic she abandoned the queue and ran to the row of pay phones, intent on contacting DS Culley and washing her hands of the problem. The sergeant wasn't at the station they said and Anabel rang off refusing to leave her name, her hands trembling as she replaced the receiver.

But Kimberley Carter's passports and cash would take some explaining when she passed through customs. One way out would be to ditch Kim's handbag in the nearest trash can before checking in. But all those dollars? And that gorgeous bag? What a waste. The glimmering sign of a currency exchange bureau caught her eye and after a few minutes' hard consideration she decided to go the whole hog and to hell with Kimberley Carter alias Martha Ferrero.

She exchanged what remained of Kim's sterling for lira, transferring everything from her own purse into the crocodile bag and tossing the plastic carrier in a litter bin. After all Kimberley did owe her that reward, didn't she? The girl in the currency kiosk obliged by coming up trumps with a large padded envelope in which Anabel covertly stuffed the passports, keys, gold lighter and the bundle of dollar bills. But the bulky organiser wrapped in the silk scarf was too much and in desperation Anabel crammed it back in Kim's bag and used a pen from the counter to address the envelope to Annie Gordon c/o her landlord Dimitri at the caff.

The accommodating girl fronting the bureau angelically sold her a book of stamps from her own supply when Anabel pleaded a heart-wringing story about almost forgetting to post her mother's birthday present. Just then the final call for her flight to Pisa boomed across the concourse. Clearly panicked by this, she fished for a further saintly gesture from the girl at the kiosk who eventually agreed to post the parcel herself in her coffee break. Anabel could hardly believe her luck and with a grin wide as the Forth Bridge thrust the wretched thing across the counter and rushed off.

Rejoining the queue and checking in her luggage took only a matter of minutes and it was only after she fastened her seatbelt and watched the grey tarmac slide away under the wheels of the plane that Anabel realised she might have been mistaken in sidestepping the police investigation. Gail would have to give Culley her address if he found out she had passed on her Zelini invitation. And if Kimberley was questioned, the theft of her expensive handbag would come to light. Did her message on the Turner House answerphone constitute blackmail? Her words, looking back on it, had been very curt. Might her anonymous demands even be regarded as criminally threatening? Though presumably, in view of the extra passport, the Carter girl would prefer not to make any official complaint while there was still a chance of settling with the finder through a private deal. Stealing an expensive handbag and spending the money was small beer compared with toting a fraudulent passport, but Anabel had practically moved heaven and earth to return everything directly, hadn't she? If questioned, she could say – quite truthfully – she didn't have Kim's home address and had only retained the bag because it was too bulky to post at the last minute. Sounded feasible. But there remained the business of not cooperating with the police by registering her presence at the fire and thus hampering their inquiries into the identification of the dead body in the loo. And there was still the question of that Zelini velvet cloak . . .

Why had she allowed herself to get sucked into all this? Kim's promise of a reward had been the bait but Anabel ruefully conceded it was her own greed that lay at the bottom of it. Being rich and honest was easy. Being dirt poor and tempted was something else.

Envy played a part. And deception came naturally. It was her specialised skill honed over years in the business of copying art works. For what purpose did her shady clients require facsimiles of their ancestral treasures? She had never asked, shutting her mind to the dodgy possibilities her takes presented. And they were good fakes. Old Philip Barclayson was an expert and he had employed her for years. But now, with the purloining of Kim's handbag and Kim's money, morality had taken a real dive.

"You are, Anabel Gordon, no better than a common pickpocket dipping wallets in Oxford Street."

Six

Tom Culley had joined the police after three years of dispiriting failure as a futures dealer. Gambling not being his forte; the Asian financial crisis sealed his fate. Joining the Met was a decision taken in desperation, a job to pay off a mountain of debts and allow him to save enough capital to emigrate. His live-in girlfriend, Gerry, packed her bags when he got the push from the City and exchanged his smooth suiting and striped shirts for a copper's uniform.

In fact, to his surprise, chasing villains proved much more exciting than being glued to the vicissitudes of the international money markets and the loss of his Morgan was small beer compared with the loss of Gerry. Her humiliating parting shots rankled, and passing his police exams became an obsession, a need to prove his worth, a means of blocking out the ugly recriminations which stained any leisure hours.

His promotion to detective sergeant had been swift. His boss, Chief Inspector Kline, an officer of the old school, sarcastic in his dealings with his new sidekick, presented a situation Tom Culley learned to live with, his hide thickened by the cheerful jibes in the police canteen which merely flicked the surface after Gerry's acerbic summary of his financial freefall.

The Zelini fire was Culley's first challenge, and the identification of the body trapped in the loo was paramount in DCI

Kline's caseload. The pathologist was not much help, his brief report giving little away. Culley checked his notes: Female, five foot eight, age approximately 35. Slim build, curly dark hair, professionally manicured nails and a naturally suntanned complexion. From holidays or residence in a warmer climate? Death due to inhalation of smoke and noxious gases, the body burnt only after death. Dental records? No other injuries. No means of identification on the lovely corpse. No wedding ring. Only jewellery a valuable ruby and diamond heart-shaped locket of modern design and probably purchased in London or Paris.

He lay in bed reviewing the situation. Abigail Griffith, the woman he had interviewed the morning after the fire, knew more than she was letting on. Eliminating the woman to whom she had passed her invitation must be the first step. Tracking down the other four mysterious entries in the visitors' book would be more difficult. Having caught the Griffith woman still wrapped in her duvet last time, a second dawn raid was called for. He had been conditioned to early rising in his City job and being one step ahead of the opposition was now an ingrained habit. Sliding long legs from the sack he looked forward to another round with the mendacious art editor. Just as soon as he'd done a couple of laps of Clapham Common to get his juices pumping.

Tom Culley in attack mode was impressive – six foot three and rugged with it, dark eyed, a narrow face graced with a nose Lord Wellington could have cloned lending an impression of intensity which Gerry had often found 'heavy'. Breaking up with Gerry was, now he looked back on it, inevitable. Geraldine Scott-Holden was a daddy's girl whose requirements were simple: cash on tap and plenty of entertainment both in bed and out on the town. While the dealing game had been on a roll Gerry could overlook the basic gravitas of Tom Culley. Stripped of a decent salary and depressed by his own failure as a hot-shot money man, the romance had definitely curdled.

Detective Chief Inspector Kline was congenitally lazy and more than happy to let his CID team do the legwork. This suited Culley down to the ground. A loner, given to hunches not always easy to accommodate in his written reports – following his nose became easier under a man like Kline. Kline wanted results – and quick. If Ms Griffith couldn't come up with a name, Culley would turn on the girls in the Zelini showroom, shake the tree a bit, make them deliver the names of the people who got hold of invites on the side.

He arrived at the block of flats where Abigail Griffith lived just as the caretaker was putting out the rubbish for collection. Culley had had a run in with this guy on his previous visit, the janitor's minty breath losing the battle with last night's booze. Denny Clapp straightened, the buttons of his boilersuit straining across his beer belly.

"Ah, Mr Clapp." Culley proffered a mocking half-salute.

"You again. Don't your lot never get tired of harassing innocent people? Ms Griffith ain't in. Tried knocking last night to remind her to put the rubbish out on the landing."

"But her car's here," Culley persisted, pointing out the red MG parked at the kerb a few yards along the street.

"How d'you know her motor?"

"I'm a detective, aren't I?" Culley retorted with a grin.

"Well, you ain't no Sherlock fucking Holmes, matey. She takes a taxi to work most days."

"This early?"

The caretaker re-lit his dog-end, regarding the obstinate flatfoot and his sopping wet mac with a curl of the lip. "OK. Suit yourself." He watched Culley ring through on the entry button and relished the man's frustration when there was no response.

"Let me inside, Clapp, and I'll bang her bloody door down. This is a woman's death I'm investigating and I'm fed up with playing footsie with you people."

"More'n me job's worth," Clapp retorted, moving off to line up the wheelie bins at the kerb. Culley grabbed the man's shoulder and pressed his face close to his ear, mouthing something which caused Clapp to flinch, clearly shaken. Culley let go and pushed Clapp towards the glassed-in lobby where a security camera whirred as they passed through. There was no lift, the carpeted stairs pegging the value of this unfashionable mock mansion block referred to in the trade as 'a walk-up'.

He rang and battered on Abigail Griffith's door with no result. "Police, open up!" he shouted in the bawling tone he had only heard on TV cop shows. Culley was not normally the battering-ram type but this woman annoyed him, deliberately wasting his time like this. Why hadn't she admitted straight off she had passed on her Zelini invitation?

Clapp stood firm, breathing heavily, and only moving away to reassure an elderly woman peering round the door of her flat across the landing, a pint of milk in her hand, her mouth agape. Culley gave up, contenting himself by posting his card through the letter box. He turned on his heel.

"Tell her I'll be back later," he muttered to Clapp over his shoulder, bounding down the stairs like a man on the run.

Checking at her office bore little fruit. In fact, her secretary was extremely agitated, the managing editor expecting Abigail Griffith to attend a conference at eleven and no message from her boss. Mavis Thompson was in Culley's view the sort of PA he'd give his pension for: fiftyish, unattractive and as professionally loyal as a trained gun dog. She wore a chic grey suit which matched the steel-rimmed spectacles. Myopic eyes swam with anxiety.

"It's not like her," she confided. "Always punctual. Never ill. She wasn't here yesterday either. I know Ms Griffith was worried about the deadine for the spring issue but, even so, not even to ring in . . ."

Culley left the building with a feeling it was not his day. He phoned through to say he was going straight on to the Zelini showroom to interview the staff and checked that there had been no overnight developments regarding the nameless corpse in the morgue. Riding roughshod over the temp in the Zelini office did, however, produce results. A tearful admission that yes, there had been some slippage with the invitation cards. Two of the women who had signed the visitors' book but whose names were not on the invitation list were swiftly eliminated from his enquiries. Now only two invitations were still a mystery and the heartfelt assurances of the typist who had sold the other two invites to a PR firm that she was innocent of syphoning off the last two missing cards rang true.

Culley asked to see the cleaning staff but they were long gone: a Mrs Miller, whose address in Battersea went into his notebook, and a Mary Maguire, who was the only cleaner trusted to deal with the workroom and its stacks of delicate fabrics and secret designs. He decided to go back to Chelsea and type up his notes while the facts were still clear in his head. Not that there was much progress in the investigation so far.

The fire inspectors came up with no evidence of arson which was at least one aspect of this baffling case out of the running. The blaze had started in the basement apparently, some sort of electrical fault, presumably caused by old wiring snaking behind the bolts of cloth stored there. Kline was out checking up on the fire victims still hospitalised, the desk sergeant reported. "Chatting up the rich and influential ladies on his patch more like," Culley retorted.

He phoned Abigail Griffith's home number several times during the day and checked regularly with her secretary. A singular rapport had sprung up between them and on his last call her anxiety was such that she invited Culley to accompany her to her boss's flat that evening after work to deliver some urgent copy.

"What if she's really out? Not just lying doggo?"

"I'm concerned she may have been taken ill . . . She left a spare set of keys here in the office," she whispered. "Gee-Gee was always worried about being locked out, Sergeant."

Culley leapt upon Miss Thompson's tentative suggestion like a lion felling his quarry, only managing to curb his avid response just in time. He offered to pick her up from the *Eve Now* building at six thirty, wondering if the woman really was delivering copy or just needed back-up to give her courage to make what might seem an intrusion into Ms Griffith's private life. No doubt the secretary was being discreet about her suspicions regarding the company her boss kept out of hours. A resident toy boy perhaps?

It was still raining, the dark clouds bringing an early twilight to the April evening as Culley parked outside Fountain Court and accompanied Miss Thompson, using the spare keys to access the foyer.

As soon as she opened the door it was obvious that, in Abigail Griffith's absence, the place had been ransacked. An amateur break-in in Culley's view – the trashing of the apartment sheer overkill, not a professional keyhole job at all. Mavis Thompson gasped, leaning weakly against the wall, her cheeks ashen. Every room was in chaos, books strewn across the floor, drawers upended, tables overturned, cushions slit and frothing with feathery innards.

Culley roughly pushed the woman back out into the hall where she collapsed on a spindly bamboo chair.

The place had been systematically trashed, even pictures torn from the walls and lying broken amid the chaos. The kitchen had been taken apart, the contents of the freezer strewn about, a pack of frozen chips emptied on to the worktop. Alarm bells rang in his head: not a common burglary after all. What were they hoping to find? Drugs?

Culley went back to recheck the front door. No broken lock. An inside job using a key or an expert lockpicker who somehow circumvented the entry phone system. On balance the caretaker was likely to have been in on it, checking the tenants' comings and goings and presumaby having keys to most, if not all, of the flats.

He assured Mavis Thompson there was no danger, the perpetrators of this ham-fisted robbery long gone. He told her to stay put while he had a last look round, checking the bathroom last, but she pulled herself together like a real pro, silently dogging his footsteps, aghast at the mayhem.

As soon as he opened the bathroom door the stench of death seeped into Culley's consciousness like a familiar ghost.

Abigail Griffith sat propped up on the lavatory, her feet tied with steel wire, flecks of dried blood staining her thick ankles where the vicious tautening of the ligature had bitten into the flesh. Her hands were handcuffed behind her back and secured to the cistern with more wire, the trussing up of the corpse the only reason it remained upright. The naked chest was brutally revealed, her blouse ripped aside, torn bra straps dangling from her lap. Mavis uttered a muted cry, half fainting with the shock.

Culley grabbed her arm, shoving her out of the windowless bathroom overheated by the old-fashioned geyser, the air thick as treacle. He drew back, anxious not to disturb the crime scene. Abigail Griffith's head with its shock of straw-like hair bowed over her chest as if she was examining the haft of what looked like an ordinary kitchen knife protruding from below her ribs. But Culley had seen knife wounds before – gaping slashes the result of gang fights on a Saturday night. That was not what took his breath away. No police experience had prepared him for this.

Her sagging breasts had been systematically scarred with cigarette burns, the torture now darkened to black dots.

Seven

Anabel emerged from Pisa airport like a butterfly emerging from a chrysalis. The sun shone, the air smelling deliciously of garlic and spring rain, and Philip Barclayson's driver waiting to whisk her and her meagre luggage to the villa. Heaven.

She greeted Rocco with glee, his Neopolitan thuggery disguised by a chauffeur's hat, massive pecs straining under his shirt. Barclayson's driver doubled as a bodyguard and within a wide radius of La Colomba Rocco had acquired a reputation not to be trifled with. He tossed the peaked cap onto the back seat and grinned, revealing a set of gnashers like tombstones, each tooth spaced from the next as if for maximum efficiency.

"Hi Rocco! Still growing, I see."

Anabel kissed the man mountain on both cheeks, standing on tip-toe, her glance wickedly flirtatious. She and Rocco were mates, an alliance forged during her three previous stays at La Colomba, their status curiously akin – Anabel's apparent acceptance as a house guest fooling nobody. Each knew their role to be no more and no less than a necessary tool Philip Barclayson would prefer to do without, his criticism of the girl's gypsyish appearance blunted by her usefulness, not to mention a grudging regard for her formidable talent

41

which he persisted in decrying for his peace of mind if not his purse.

Anabel bounced into the front passenger seat of the big Fiat, punching Rocco's massive biceps in sheer pleasure at being here. In Italy. In April. Far from London and the sheer brutalities of life on the edge.

The countryside flew past like a dream sequence, the sunshine sparkling off the wet roof tiles as if the scenery was a painted backdrop freshly varnished for her pleasure. Barclayson's villa was only thirty kilometres from Pisa, Lucca, her very favourite medieval walled delight, being its nearest town. The old connoisseur had bought shrewdly, the elegant sixteenth-century house now immaculately restored, its lengthy corridors and extensive wall space presenting a framework for his collection of nineteenth-century high art. Originally purchased as a winter retreat Barclayson now rarely left La Colomba, forays to the auction houses of New York, London and Monte Carlo dwindling as the years took their toll on the elderly reprobate.

The villa never ceased to enchant her despite misgivings about her host, his hospitality swinging wildly between charming exuberance and the open dislike of any who dared outstay his welcome. Anabel braced herself for Barclayson's initial overwhelming affection, knowing that before a week or, with luck, a fortnight had passed the old man would become bored and demand that Alys conjure up new house guests to amuse him. Fortunately, she had not been invited on the strength of her entertainment value.

La Colomba had been reclaimed from near dereliction and now presented a combination of old and new, including an orangery, plus a gym and swimming pool secluded in an annexe. The villa itself remained as lovely as ever, a classic residence standing at an angle from the road and almost invisible behind mature terraced gardens bounded by ilex avenues. One of the nicer aspects of staying with Barclayson was the ever-changing complement of visitors, both young decoratives and eminent oldies, a range of guests by no means restricted to arty types. This fragile balancing act of hospitality was buoyed up by the lady of the house, a middle-aged American from Oklahoma called Alys Trimmer. No-one was ever quite sure how Philip Barclayson had acquired the devotion of Alys Trimmer. If ever she had been she certainly was no longer his mistress. In her youth she must have been a stunner and even now, fiftyish and prematurely white-haired, the lithe movements and conversational elegance lent her a grace both in looks and manner that was fascinating.

Alys ran the house with a sleight of hand Anabel found astonishing. The woman spirited away a charmless guest with the agility of a conjurer, the victim himself feeling no pain, enchanted by Alys's smooth witchcraft as hostess, warm-hearted companion and chief conspirator in the Keep Philip Happy team. Every rich man, thought Anabel, should have a woman like Alys Trimmer.

The car drew up at the colonnade which defined the central block of the house. Anabel jumped out of the car to be fiercely hugged by Alys ready and waiting in the cool shade, a table laid for a late lunch, an open bottle of Frascati at her elbow.

"Darling! How was the flight? You look pale, honey. We must cosset you a little before Philip starts badgering. He's already got together a whole raft of drawings to discuss with you."

They sipped wine, their laughter penetrating the inner courtyard like the chirping of starlings under the eaves. The hot scent of rosemary hung in the air attracting a cloud of bees to the edge of the terrace.

"Philip's having his siesta. We've got hours before tea. I want to hear *all* your news."

Alys wore a black linen dress, expensively simple, probably Armani, her gestures expressive as any Italian mamma after years in Tuscany ministering to the whims of her irrascible partner. Alys was the eighth wonder of the world in Anabel's view, her seamless affability never disclosing any suspicion of brittleness despite the organisational demands of La Colomba.

The afternoon slid by, Alys ticking off the roll call of guests, warning Anabel of their *placement* in the current house party.

"Our most tiring quartet are Rocky Minola and her new husband and—"

"Rocky Minola! The tinned baby-food queen?"

Alys nodded. 'Hubby mark IV is actually quite nice. A Prussian princeling called Felix von something or other. But she bullies him dreadfully so he gets a little sulky at times."

"The others?"

"Oh a sweet young man called Freddie Knight, an actor apparently though I don't think anyone's ever heard of him. Rocky picked him up in Venice and persuaded Philip to let him join us. It won't last, of course. The boy stupidly made a pass at Rocco the other evening and as you know Philip never misses a thing."

"Who else?"

"Another art critic, I'm afraid. Probably useful to you if you play your cards right, sweetie. But, oh my, deadly dull, Anabel. Quite necrotic in fact. James Royd-Chiddingstone. A big noise at the Institute I'm told. You must have seen his stuff in *Apollo*."

Anabel flushed, recalling the man's icy retort to her own unguarded comment at a book launch for the latest biography of Whistler, written, as bad luck would have it, by a protégé of Royd-Chiddingstone's. She comforted herself with the thought that these people never remembered small fry like Anabel Gordon who had, in fact, gatecrashed the publisher's bash at the instigation of her last lost love, Greg Stainsburton, a shit of the first water, a man who still owed her the money for his taxi fare home that night, dammit.

Later as she unpacked in her room, the sheer bliss of the forthcoming month at La Colomba seeped into her bones like the solace of very old and very rare cognac.

The room Alys had assigned to her lay at the western end of the villa overlooking the curve in the road from Lucca before one was confronted by the rusty gates of La Colomba. The room supposedly did not enjoy a favourable aspect, its low beams gathering the heat of the afternoon sun into a golden ball which penetrated every corner. But Anabel loved it. The authentic rustic furnishings never ceased to delight, the functional shower room its only modernity. This room, which Alys always kept aside for her, was the nearest to paradise Anabel had ever encountered. Only the bleak recollection of her afternoon with Ronnie in that god-awful council flat in Kings Cross clouded the moment, emphasising the undeniable truth that Ronnie's world was the substance and *this* the shadow of life as it really was.

After a shower she lay on the bed wrapped in a towel, suddenly depressed, watching a lizard zig-zag across the wall. It was true. She had run away from reality. She had stepped into La Colomba like Alice through the Looking Glass to where everything instantly became both magical and menacing. Why was she here? Why continue to dance to Philip Barclayson's tune, to trot out his dubious commissions?

"Isn't it about time, Anabel Gordon, you broke the mirror and stopped pretending the reflection is actuality?"

Eight

Tom Culley reluctantly handed over the investigation of the Griffith murder to the local Superintendent, a man called Ackroyd, an acquaintance of Culley's own boss, DCI Kline. Bad news. Kline's instructions were clear. "Make your statement and get out of Ackroyd's light – it's off our patch."

Having stumbled upon the body of Abigail Griffith trussed up like a turkey whose feathers had been cruelly singed, Culley was reluctant to let the thing go. But Ackroyd was adamant.

"Just a bungled raid that went belly up, then from sheer frustration at finding nothing worth pinching ended up in sexual sadism. Bastards probably on drugs. Seen it all before, lad. Don't lose any sleep over it. Leave it to us."

"Any evidence on the security video in the foyer, sir?"

Ackroyd sighed like a politician humouring a persistent heckler.

"I thought Kline told you to keep your nose out of it?"

"Yes, sir. But you see I discovered the body in the course of conducting my own investigation. Into another matter," he quickly added. "Any information you have may have a bearing on our own inquiry."

"Look, sergeant. I haven't got all fucking night to argue with you. This is a murder hunt and Kline tells me your brief

47

was just to check out some poncy invitation list. Hardly big time, eh?"

"With respect, sir, *we* have a body too. And until it's identified—"

"Just piss off, d'you hear? Let me get on with my job and if there's any fallout which answers any of *your* questions my sergeant here will fill you in. OK?"

The plain clothes detective standing to attention at Ackroyd's shoulder gave a barely perceptible wink. Culley tactically withdrew, leaving the two of them to pick their way through the havoc left by Griffith's killer.

As he left the building he caught sight of a tearful Mavis Thompson being led to a police car parked at the kerb, presumably being escorted home. He glanced at his watch. It was already after ten and he'd had nothing to eat all day. Reluctantly he admitted his gripes were as nothing compared with the state of shock the dead woman's secretary must be experiencing. He sprinted over to the waiting panda car and, gently elbowing Mavis Thompson out of earshot, took the driver aside and flashed his ID.

"The Super suggested I took Miss Thompson home as you're so shorthanded. It's on my way. Right?"

He smiled at the woman who, like himself, had been grilled like someone caught redhanded at the crime scene. Their interviews had been conducted separately in the caretaker's office, Clapp himself having been hauled off to the station to 'help the police with their inquiries'. Having a criminal record, albeit way back, left the poor bloody caretaker in the firing line.

"My car's just here, Miss Thompson. I'm sorry you got dragged into this. I feel responsible for you being here in the first place."

She stumbled along beside him, wordless with fright, but the wan smile she threw at Culley as he settled her in the passenger seat spoke volumes.

It was only when they were caught up in a traffic jam that she found her voice, her tremulous phrases almost inaudible.

"I *knew* something was wrong. I would have called in anyway just to make sure she was all right. Thank God you were with me, Sergeant Culley. I shall never be able to forget that last sight of poor Gee-Gee. And the horrible thing is she had been left like that for over twenty-four hours. I should have gone over on Thursday – I might have saved her life if I'd been there. Those people who tortured her are fiends! Fiends from hell."

"Please don't dwell on it, Miss Thompson. We did our best." Culley made an effort to bring a new direction to their conversation. "The Superintendent seems to think she was targeted. Ms Griffith had no particular valuables you were aware of, did she?"

"Jewellery, you mean?"

"Anything. I can't think why else the place was so thoroughly ransacked, can you?"

Miss Thompson shook her head, miserably aware that she did, in fact, know very little about her employer's circumstances.

"Was there anyone else with spare keys? A cleaning woman? There was no forced entry."

She brightened, clutching at this as if she had, at last, something to contribute.

"Absolutely not. A cleaning firm was contracted to call at the house every Thursday evening. She let them in herself and they stayed for an hour – she never allowed people in her home when she wasn't there."

"And you told Superintendent Ackroyd this?"

"Oh yes. But he wasn't interested. He said they had evidence on the video, a film pinpointing the time the two burglars arrived, well after the cleaners had left, a recording of one of the men's discussion with Gee-Gee on the entry phone. And the cleaners went on somewhere else afterwards, their movements are fully documented he said. I'm glad of that. One doesn't like to think people one has learned to trust would do such a thing."

Culley smoothly changed gear, nodding encouragement as he negotiated the Hogarth roundabout.

"Oh yes," she continued, "it was nothing to do with the cleaning firm, they have been cleared. It was a fellow in a bike messenger's outfit – crash helmet, a scarf, you know . . ."

Culley's hopes plummeted. "Hardly recognisable then. But Ackroyd confirmed there were two suspects?"

"Oh, absolutely. I saw the video myself. The Superintendent wanted to know if I recognised the messenger."

"You?"

"I often express copy and proofs to Ms Griffith at home, especially if we're coming up to a deadline."

"You *knew* this bloke?"

"No! I swear he wasn't any of our usual boys. He went up to the entry phone all wrapped up as they are and spoke quite clearly. An educated voice on the recording. Said he had some photographs Mr St Clair urgently wanted her to caption before Friday."

"Mr St Clair?"

"Our managing editor. A very demanding person. It wouldn't be the first time he pursued staff at home. That was why Gee-Gee absolutely refused to have a fax machine at her flat. Said her life would never be her own if you let Mr St Clair have open sesame day and night."

"Ah, yes, I see what you mean. I had a boss like that at my last job."

In the course of her recital Mavis Thompson had visibly brightened, abandoning her formal references to her boss, now only Gee-Gee, a name privately shared with the typing staff and an indication that Culley was now, since their mutual discovery, an insider like herself.

"What else did Ackroyd say? He had no time for me, I'm afraid. Unfortunately, a sort of professional jealousy often exists between different CID teams. It can lead to a terrible lack of communication. Ms Griffith let this bike messenger into the foyer then? Wouldn't she normally go down to the ground floor herself to sign for a package?"

"Gee-Gee was rather lazy, I'm afraid. It was not unusual to have express deliveries late in the evening. Media people work round the clock when it comes to deadlines and asking the biker to come straight up would not faze her. She knew most of them you see."

"But you saw a second man on the film?"

"Yes! That was what was so odd. Of course, when Gee-Gee told the first man to come up she had no idea she was admitting two of them and that they were not the usual chaps."

"And presumably there were no urgent photographs to see anyway?"

"I can't answer that. You'll have to ask Mr St Clair and he's generally at his weekend place in the country by this time even when an issue is about to go to press. Still, he may be working tomorrow."

Culley frowned. No doubt about it, Ackroyd was playing his cards very close to his chest, pooling information not an item on his agenda, not with a new boy like himself anyhow. Never showed *me* any bloody security video, he fumed.

"But if the thieves knew all about this, someone must have tipped them off about Ms Griffith's normal working practices – they watched the cleaning firm leave and then moved in. Bundling her inside her own flat as soon as she opened the door for the biker would be child's play. And that flat wasn't a plywood modern place, was it? Those pre-war blocks were built to last. Soundproof. No-one complained about any noise, screaming and so on, did they?"

"Perhaps she was gagged before she had a chance to scream. And they had a knife. Also, that bathroom is at the middle of the apartment – no windows. You see, that would make a difference, wouldn't it?"

Culley grinned, wondering if, after all, his Miss Thompson would prove to be a Miss Marple in disguise. They drew up outside her house, a maisonette in Chiswick, a nice location overlooking the river. Since leaving Hampstead she had regained her composure and declined his offer to see her inside.

"I live with my sister. I shall be perfectly safe, I assure you. No need to worry, sergeant. May I say how much I appreciate your kindness? Being driven home in a police vehicle would have alarmed my sister quite dreadfully. I'm sure she's awfully worried as it is. I said I would be late home but naturally assumed calling in to see Gee-Gee after work would take no time at all and I have been unable to telephone her since. Oh dear."

He watched her being greeted on the doorstep and when the two women had gone inside drove back to the murder scene, intent on collaring Ackroyd's sidekick who seemed a decent enough bloke and more likely to be cooperative with the big man out of the way. In fact Sergeant Lee had already been dispatched to augment the interrogation of the caretaker, poor miserable Clapp, and Ackroyd himself was still shovelling the debris inside the flat. However, the constable in the foyer was in a chatty mood, eager to savour the gritty details.

"What's this chap Clapp done time for then? Kevin said he's got a record."

"Rape. Years ago. But that sort of stuff sticks like fly paper. Ackroyd won't let go in a hurry. Funny thing was I had my doubts about that slimy sod when I called here before."

"You was checking up on another inquiry I 'eard. Rape?"

"No. A routine matter. But the caretaker was jamming things up for no obvious reason so I trawled through on the offchance and struck gold. Once I found out about the rape case in Liverpool I had a handle on the bloke when I needed some cooperation."

They chatted at the kerbside but nothing new came to light. Culley hung about hoping something would break but the doc had been late arriving and eventually Culley gave up, his stomach growling in audible complaint. He sloped off for a curry, the spicy wodge driving out any lingering enthusiasm for squeezing any more info from Ackroyd's merry men.

Next morning he presented himself at the *Eve Now* building and insisted on seeing someone in charge. After flexing some official muscle the receptionist admitted St Clair had returned from the country with ill grace and was now prowling the art department in a foul temper. She rang through, goggle-eyed at the possible implications of a CID man's insistence on an immediate meeting with the venomous managing editor. On a Saturday morning too.

Of course St Clair made him wait and when Culley was eventually shown into the impressive office it was soon pointed out that the murder of one of his editors had already been upstaged by more pressing items: ie the production of an issue of one of the UK's major monthly magazines. Harvey

St Clair wore slacks and a cashmere pullover just to emphasise his diligence in working over the weekend. He sat behind a mahogany desk backed by a panoramic view of the river, the sky opalescent. He didn't waste time on niceties.

"Look here, sergeant. I've already spoken to your Superintendent this morning."

"He's been here?" Culley failed to disguise his surprise, Ackroyd not having struck him as a mover and shaker.

"Telephoned. He's sending another man, a Sergeant Lee, in later. And Sergeant Lee had the courtesy to make an appointment! You lot seem to have got your wires crossed. But as I've already explained, my association with Ms Griffith did not extend to confidences about her financial affairs. How would I know what sort of baubles she kept at home?"

"She worked here for some years I understand?"

"Almost eight. But even so—"

"Pardon me, Mr St Clair, but I really think you may have some useful information without realising it. My inquiry is more concerned with her social circle, you see. Ms Griffith passed on a private invitation to a woman friend and in order to follow up all possible leads it is imperative I find out about her personal contacts in the office."

"Ask Mavis Thompson. Her secretary. She'll be in on Monday. I can't be expected to know all the tittle tattle that goes on round here."

"I have already spoken to that lady. In fact, Miss Thompson was with me when the body was discovered. She knows nothing about Ms Griffith's men friends or much about her private life at all it seems."

"Men friends!" St Clair let out what could only be described as hollow laughter. "If you're supposed to be a detective you haven't even got to first base with that filly. Men friends! The only 'friend' I've ever caught her with was a total fluke when my wife and I were off on a quiet break in Paris last month. Clocked Gee-Gee and her partner in this dinky little hotel near Fontainebleau. I made sure she didn't spot me, of course. And I never breathed a word about it afterwards, of course. The repercussions might have been heavy."

"A partner? Someone you recognised?"

"Oh yes. I was so intrigued I checked it out with the hotel manager afterwards – surprising what a little reward will reveal. Not that the stupid Frog knew what a bombshell he was sitting on, of course. Just to make sure, I managed to take a couple of snapshots while they were canoodling over breakfast on the terrace."

Culley waited, recognising in St Clair a man who had reluctantly harboured a delicious titbit of gossip for too long and was relishing the excuse – a citizen's duty in view of the official nature of the interview, of course – to let slip a hint of scandal as newsworthy as any journalist might hope to stumble upon. St Clair privately shuffled his options. If he was unwilling to write the story himself there were others out there in the shark pool who would recompense him handsomely for the tip-off and with an undertaking of witholding the source he would be safe. His mouth had clearly been sealed so far but with Griffith so spectacularly dead who knew what opportunities would present themselves?

"You were saying, Mr St Clair . . ."

"This horrific murder was just a burglary gone wrong, the Superintendent assures me. Thugs who overdid the persuasion, nothing whatsoever to do with my art editor's private affairs. Ah well, in the strictest confidence, of course, and not to be made public at any point of this inquiry, the 'partner' to whom I referred was, of course, a lady of distinction. A public figure, in fact – fortunately the manager of the hotel was totally unaware of the identity of his important guest."

"Ms Griffith was involved in a lesbian relationship? You're sure?"

"Of course. We all knew Gee-Gee was one of those. Such things are hardly a secret these days. But the astonishing thing was not Griffith's sexual inclinations but her lover's. The person who was sharing her hotel room is a member of the government and certainly no-one who could survive 'outing'. Men in the public gaze can sometimes get away with it in these enlightened times but women, ah, that's more problematical."

"And this lady's name?"

St Clair's mouth clamped, prissy lines radiating from a perfect O. "Ah well, Sergeant Culley, that would be telling tales and I'm certain it has absolutely no bearing on your current inquiry. I think you should close the file on my late colleague's private affairs and concentrate on the muggers. I have been speaking off the record and will deny any reference to it you dare to make but, to put your mind at rest, the identity of the distinguished minister is safe with me."

Nine

A lys Trimmer's efforts to slip a few days R & R into Anabel's visit before Philip Barclayson claimed his pound of flesh were unavailing. In fairness, the imminent departure to Paris of Philip's friend Royd-Chiddingstone didn't help.

"Philip needs James to see your sketches before he goes on Tuesday. He's chairman of a high-profile panel meeting the Government lawyers about opening up the French art market to international auction houses. They're dragging their feet as usual. Too much to lose."

"What do you mean?"

"Under Gallic law French public notaries have enjoyed the exclusive right to organise auctions. The big art houses are pushing VIPs like James to insist the French reform this legislation which is already considered illegal by the European Commission. Luxurious Parisian premises have already been set up as auction rooms and as soon as the British get the go-ahead the big boys will move in. But argument about compensation for the loss of the monopoly will naturally be protracted." Alys's hollow laughter struck a cynical note unusual in itself.

"Big money involved? Philip's investing in this?"

Alys swiftly resumed a businesslike manner, cutting short

any further chit chat. "That's beside the point. James will be back in Venice in a few days and we have all been invited to a big party at Rocky's palazzo. She wants you to come."

"Me?"

She laughed. "Well it's probably our little Hun's idea. Felix has taken a real shine to you, honey. Wouldn't you enjoy a few days in Venice? You don't have to stay at Rocky's gloomy old ratheap. I've a tiny pied-à-terre of my own near the Rialto you're welcome to use. You could work there undisturbed, away from Philip's badgering."

"You're not coming?"

"No. Philip's staying with Rocky and I've got a million things to do here."

"Gosh, Alys. That sounds fabulous! Are you sure you don't mind me using your place? I've never been to Venice before."

"Great! That's settled then. I'll talk to you about it later. Just as soon as I've kicked out Freddie Knight."

"He's leaving too?"

"Yes. But I've got a nice young researcher arriving on Sunday. Canadian. Writing a scandalous biography of Anthony Blunt."

"Philip *knew* Blunt?"

"Of course. Poor Anthony was much admired for his expertise. A pity about the other thing." Alys glanced away, mixed emotions flitting across her mobile features like scudding rainclouds.

"Tell me again. What's the drill here?"

Alys snapped back into focus, smiling in that enigmatic Giaconda way which always made Anabel uneasy.

"Firstly, James and Philip want to go over your Italian sketches in the library. He has a particular interest in those etching plates you had made up."

58

"Today?"

"This afternoon. OK?"

"Fine by me. But some time I'd like to slip into Lucca to buy some postcards." And make a few phonecalls she thought to herself, unwilling to ring Ronnie from La Colomba, anxious not to get dragged into any awkward explanations. And there was still the problem of Kimberley Carter's stuff now presumably shoved behind the counter at Dimitri's caff awaiting her return. She owed him a warning. Also she should ring the Twiggy girl's mobile number and reassure the silly bitch that her things were safe. But what the hell! Hadn't she already turned cartwheels trying to return that bloody handbag? And she'd promised to send a card to Abigail Griffith with her new address.

Anabel thrust all these knotty problems into a mental attic and forced herself to attend to Alys's request. It was never wise to disregard Alys Trimmer's directions. Accidentally putting a spanner in those oiled works would wreak havoc on the smooth running of La Colomba and fouling up Alys's clockwork arrangements could only bring Philip's wrath upon her head, God help her. There would be no time for swanning around Lucca until after the weekend.

Her afternoon staked out like a vestal virgin between the two elderly art critics left her head spinning. Their microscopic perusal of the precious sketches and etchings she had guarded on the flight from London was on a par with being done over with a nit comb by the school nurse.

But luck was on her side. Just as the clock struck four and Alys wheeled in the tea trolley, Rocco arrived back from the airport with the freighted Whistler portrait. Abandoning their interrogations, James and Philip leapt upon the painting which Rocco had obligingly unpacked leaving only the inner linen wrappings for the old boys to tear apart. Alys stood back, her elegant head poised, alert as a carrion crow.

In the subdued afternoon shadows the portrait of the young girl with all its tonal subtleties glowed dully, the set of the sitter's sulky mouth heartrending in its childish petulance. Anabel breathed easy. Even Philip must admit it was a superb copy. Certainly her best work. But why did he need it? He had never commissioned a famous facsimile before. His requirements had always been for obscure nineteenth-century artists, little known daubs of, to Anabel's mind, dubious merit. Parking herself in the Tate hour after hour, reproducing the stubborn lines of the child's bored attendance to the ever-demanding and eccentric Whistler, had been a labour of love.

Philip was restless in front of the large portrait Rocco had placed on an easel to catch the fading light, grabbing James's arm in excitement, tracing the brush strokes with a gnarled finger, incandescent with glee. James was more serious. He stood back, his large head tilted, a thin smile playing about his lips. Anabel glanced from one to another, wondering what the joke was. James turned to her.

"You have caught the mood splendidly, dear girl. You did realise, of course, that Whistler made that poor child pose for weeks, reducing her to tears on more than one occasion. And just when the darling moppet thought her ordeal was over, he would scrape it all off and start again!"

Alys joined in, emboldened by the frivolity the success of Anabel's picture had brought.

"Holy moly! Really? I had read somewhere that Whistler took so long over one of his child portraits that other people's kids were dragged into posing in rotation until the original subject returned from America – the mother of five children – and the portrait was still unfinished. Could it be true?"

"Absolutely!"

Everyone laughed, unable to take their eyes off the picture of the delicate little person in her best party dress.

Philip darted forward, hoarse with excitement. "And poor little Cicely Alexander certainly suffered. But oh, for what generations of adulation. A triumph, Anabel, my dear. Alys, take this wretched tea away and fetch some champagne. We must toast this reincarnation of Jimmy Whistler's moth of a child."

The festive atmosphere continued to pervade the dinner table that evening, Rocky Minola and her nice princeling baffled by their hosts' unexpected air of celebration. Freddie Knight got steadily drunk and said nothing at all.

One of the unexpected charms of staying at La Colomba was the rustic cuisine. Far from prodding her cook to construct impressive banquets for Philip's important guests, Alys presented them with the very best of local ingredients in season incorporated into traditional Tuscan dishes. This added enormously to the delights of the visit, reintroducing jaded palates to delicious rural fare, lending an entirely false impression of simple hospitality.

Dinner that night comprised honey-glazed pork with fennel, Philip wickedly assuring Felix, the elderly Prussian, of the herb's aphrodisiacal powers, an aside Alys greeted with raised eyebrow. She hastened to invite everyone to take their coffee and dessert on to the terrace, a tactical manoeuvre not entirely occasioned by the presence of their American guest of honour, Rocky Minola.

Seated in the scented twilight, lulled by the chirrup of insects in the rose garden, Anabel fought a losing battle with sated pleasure to stay lively, her eyelids growing heavier by the minute, while Alys was still managing at the end of a long day to keep all those tricky social balls in the air.

Anabel's anxieties, dulled by too much champagne, only resurfaced as she lay in bed that night mulling over the latest commission Philip had laid before her. It was much more daunting than any full-blown oil portrait, and much more dangerous. Was it time she pulled out? Took her fee and crawled back to her hole in Brixton? Her head hurt. Best thing would be to take everything La Colomba had to offer and at least grab the unforseen break in Venice. Decide later. In a flat on her own, away from the constant demands of being both guest and employee, she could weigh things up. Feel free to dance to her own tune for once.

It was only when the new house guest, the literary researcher Matt Randall, flew in from London on Sunday that she caught sight of the weekend newspapers dumped by the garbage outside the kitchen. Matt had used his papers to double wrap a Waterford crystal vase, a hostess gift for Alys.

It was the grainy photograph that first caught her eye: the broad flat features, the little black eyes spiky with mascara, the ragged cap of bleached hair. Abigail Griffith.

She smoothed out the newsprint with trembling fingers and read, in stomach-churning detail, of the beating poor Gee-Gee had endured before the muggers finished her off with a knife from her own kitchen drawer.

Anabel gagged, nauseous, crumpling the soiled paper to her chest as she flew back to her room to digest this appalling blow in private. Why? Why go to such lengths? What did Abigail Griffith ever have that was worth killing for?

Ten

Sergeant Culley circled the Griffith murder investigation like a lone hyena waiting for the lions to finish feeding, nervous of drawing attention to himself in the light of his own boss's insistence that Superintendent Ackroyd was absolutely on the right track: she had simply been the victim of a mugging which, through the drug-induced frenzy of her attackers, went just too far. Ackroyd had only issued the barest facts to the press, omitting the cigarette burns, concentrating on the beating the poor woman had received before the fatal stab wound.

Lee, Ackroyd's sergeant, watched Culley sniffing round and after a few days, when the steam had gone out of Ackroyd's enthusiasm, allowed Culley to re-examine the crime scene, dogging his steps like a bridesmaid.

"Look here, Culley, what's your problem? Anyone can see these two freaks turned the place over. Who knows *what* they found? Or what they were looking for? Anyway, what was the stupid woman holding out for?"

"Perhaps she didn't *have* anything."

"Sez you!"

"Just look at the facts, man. She wasn't earning such a fat salary, didn't go in for flashy diamonds and, as far as anyone could see, wasn't doing drugs apart from the odd snort. Why would two expert thieves go to all that trouble?"

63

"What trouble?"

"Well, they weren't your average opportunists, were they? Targeted the poor cow. Even sussed out the name of her managing editor, St Clair, so she'd have no qualms about opening up to accept delivery of copy from the magazine. All points to someone in the know."

"Obviously the fucking caretaker. Stands to reason. He thought it might end up some sort of gang rape. Not a robbery at all."

Culley paused in his aimless circuit of the ransacked flat, eyeing Lee with interest.

"Has Clapp admitted that?"

"Well, he wouldn't, would he? But if as you say the woman had nothing worth pinching why bust the place up?"

"It wasn't a bungled rape – no evidence of that in the forensic report. You sure the cleaning mob have been thoroughly checked out?"

Lee nodded morosely, wishing now he had kept this interfering know-all on the doorstep.

"No joy there, Culley. They were long-term employees, all women who, having dusted every inch of the place for more than three years, would be the last to assume it was worth sacking."

Culley stood in the bathroom doorway mesmerised by the dark bloodstains obscenely splashed across the floor. He turned, feeling his frustration build up, knowing he was losing it. He forced a grin, giving Ackroyd's gofer a friendly punch in the shoulder as he passed him on the way out.

"Any hope of me getting access to her papers once Ackroyd's through? Telephone bills, letters, diary . . . ? I still haven't traced this mate of hers who Griffith passed the Zelini invite to. I'm trying to whittle it down, the girls in her office swear they weren't involved."

"You Chelsea lot still not identified the stiff caught in the fire?" Lee blew a ripe raspberry. "Blimey, Culley, if you can't even sort that one out no wonder Ackroyd wants you out from under his feet." He sniggered. But Tom Culley had heard it all before, in the canteen – an echo of the sniper fire his ex-girlfriend had aimed at his balls when he got fired from the bank, bitterness distilled from relief that someone else's head was rolling. The Germans had a word for it: *schadenfreude*.

He drove away from Fountain Court and headed back to the Zelini residence behind Harrods. He reckoned Ackroyd would soon get tired of playing dog in the manger over the Griffith affair. Culley would just have to bide his time. There were clues to the victim's private life lying under all that rubble in the flat, Culley was sure of it. And the key to identifying the anonymous corpse in the mortuary was, he knew for a fact, to be found in Griffith's papers. Why else would she say nothing when he first interviewed her about the fire, not admitting that she knew the person who had faked her signature in the visitors' book? It could only be the same female to whom she had passed her Zelini invitation in the first place. Why else refuse to come clean? What was so shady that she didn't want the charred remains to be identified?

Tom Culley ran down the area steps to knock at the tradesmen's entrance, wondering if the lady of the house had yet returned from Italy to sort out the ruins of her fashion house.

A maid of sorts opened the door, a black girl wearing a pink nylon overall, overimpressed, in fact positively awestruck by the ID Culley flashed at her. He demanded Wiffin, quick march, no messing. She closed the door leaving him standing in the dank basement area like an unpaid milkman.

After five or six minutes the butler let him himself in,

giving Culley pause for thought. Wiffin was now all ironed out, cleanshaven and smelling powerfully of brilliantine. In work mode he was altogether a different species from off-duty Wiffin tucked up in his nice little snug with his vodka and telly.

Wiffin shouted at the girl to make herself scarce. "Finish that bloody unpacking Madame keeps bleating about!" She scuttled off, disappearing up the back stairs like an overwound clockwork bunny.

Wiffin lit a cigarette, eyeing Culley with undisguised rancour.

"Well?"

"Just a few more questions, sir."

"Look, matey, I'm well out of patience with you lot. Can't you get it into your thick skull that I was just the mug on the door? If you keep coming here for tête-à-têtes with yours truly people will get the idea we're getting married."

Culley grinned, Wiffin's bullying not a patch on the rough ride he was used to from DCI Kline and certainly not in the Superintendent's league. Funny thing was all three were hatched from the same batch in a way, Wiffin's years as a prison warder tarring him with the same brush. Culley hoped promotion wouldn't afflict him like that. He'd better watch himself: acting Mr Big with the poor kid who'd opened the Zelini back door wasn't a good sign.

"Shall we sit down for a moment, sir?

"No point. Madame's back. Can't waste time down here with you and anyway I'm in no mood for your quiz shows, Culley."

"Just as you like. I can see your point, sir. Madame Zelini's not an understanding employer in work hours I suppose. We'll drive down to the station then, shall we? Make it official? This is a suspicious death which occurred on her premises we're investigating, Mr Wiffin, and you are a witness and possibly a suspect." Culley gave him another swipe. "We've yet to establish who started the fire." Wiffin stiffened. It was all lies but a man like Wiffin was an old war horse: needed a crack on the rump to get him going. And he had been, once the last customer had been admitted, on his own on the ground floor that night . . .

"All right. Five minutes."

They moved into Wiffin's back room, shutting the door.

"You see all these regular clients coming and going, don't you? Any of them entertained here? Special friends of Madame's, say? Some sort of private dining club for instance?" Culley splashed in at the deep end. "You see, I've been told that Madame has interesting parties. Orgies?"

"What bloody rubbish! Only special friends who get inside the door here are respectable ladies. Orgies? Where do you dig up all this dirt, Culley?"

"I heard there were girly dos here," he lied, waiting for the butler to fall for it.

Wiffin grunted, finally admitting, "Lezzies is no big deal these days, mate, specially in the fashion lark." He looked defensive, professional discretion fighting the redneck in him, daring Culley to snigger.

"But of course not. But you and I are men of the world not narrow-minded old farts like your average bloke next door. Question is, do you think this lady who got fried could have been one of Madame's special friends? Someone Madame herself invited and whom she, for one reason or another, wishes not to be associated with?"

"You've lost me there, sergeant. My guess is the tart caught in the fire was brought in by someone else, not Madame, some other bird with reason to lie low." Culley sighed. Win some, lose some.

"As a matter of fact there is someone but she's dead too. Funny that. Ms Griffith. You may have spotted it in the papers. A mugging. She wasn't at the sale herself but someone signed in for her. Under your nose. All part of this female network I'm trying to sort out. A sort of witches' circle, all loosely connected if you get my drift. Look here, Mr Wiffin, can't you tell me if Madame had any VIP customers here at her house? People in the public eye? Someone interesting you recognise from the telly, a woman politician for instance?"

"Don't watch the news much meself. Same old claptrap. Mind you, there *was* someone Madame made a bit of a song and dance over. She'd been introduced by another customer but for the life of me I can't remember her name. Faces, now, I'm a bleeding Memory Man with faces. But names . . . Sorry."

"Well, think about it, Mr Wiffin. We're going in circles on this case. My inspector's howling for results. If I don't produce a name shortly he's going on the telly, one of those 'Crimewatch' appeals, with a photofit of the reconstructed face of the burnt-out corpse. All guesswork, if you ask me, but it might ring bells with the general public."

Wiffin looked startled, quite put-out in fact. Tom Culley closed his notebook, miserably aware that he was probably flogging a dead horse. A telephone rang upstairs, loud and insistent. Wiffin pushed him to the door, adjusting his stiff collar, visibly sweating. A worried man.

"Look, I've got to go. Big pow-wow upstairs tonight," he said. "Madame's business partner and their lawyers getting their heads together to sort out the damage."

Culley buttoned his jacket. "Partner?"

"Big noise called Turner. One of them developers. Got ritzy

tower blocks going up all over London. Wouldn't surprise me if he closed her down altogether after this and then we'll all be out on the street."

"You're talking about Raymond Turner? Turner Developments?"

"Shush! Keep it under your hat. Supposed to be – what do you call it – a sleeping partner. That's right. Sleeping fucking tiger if you ask me."

Eleven

Culley decided to go back to the station and try to catch up with the paperwork. His desk occupied a slot near the coffee machine, usefully hemmed in with old filing cabinets. A poinsettia left over from Christmas was spasmodically revived by WPC Wendy Teller but its days were numbered, its yellowing leaves falling with ever greater frequency, its death rattle practically audible.

Culley disliked being deskbound but there was nothing for it: reports, expense sheets, clear-up crime statistics could be ignored no longer. Kline, a born-again administrator, seemed to revel in all this analysis of figures. Culley having spent years trapped in a dealing room frantically assessing the odds, was left psychologically allergic to Kline's enthusiasm for numbers, finding the mean streets infinitely more absorbing.

The girls at the station had more or less given up on their handsome new CID sergeant. At first he had been a natural target and the fact that the man had a classy flat of his own hinted at a moneyed background, intriguing in itself. But Culley's friendly approach ultimately disclosed limits and, without actually putting a line under relationships at work, the female element of Kline's little kingdom soon got the message. But Culley had let slip barbed references to a former girlfriend and despite ribald speculation in the canteen it had to be admitted that the bloke was definitely not gay.

Kline himself had made careful enquiries about his new sergeant's comfortable circumstances and had come up with nothing even remotely supporting any notion that his sidekick was on the take. Bent coppers were Kline's ultimate terror – a police bribery investigation had destroyed a former boss and left the Chief Inspector with a desperate determination to keep the fluff from under his bed.

In fact, as he managed to winkle out, Culley had bought his bachelor pad in Clapham long before joining the Force, the mortgage covered by renting the place out for years while he had worked through the ranks. Despite Kline's discreet enquiries, the flat was now reclaimed on what seemed a totally bona fide basis. What a burden it is to have a suspicious nature! But Kline was a belt-and-braces man.

Aware that his credentials both as a possible date and as a run-of-the-mill sergeant had not entirely passed muster, Culley carried on as usual – a bit of a loner, a bit 'intense' as they put it, but basically a decent sort of bloke. His trump card was his place on the station's football team, a mixed bag of weekend kickers where Culley's deft footwork paid off. If only for the kudos of a winning side, Kline was far from anxious to lose Culley and kept his bawl-outs within reasonable bounds.

Culley himself was increasingly worried about the identification of the corpse dragged from the Zelini fire. Why the mystery? Off the record the poor cow had been dubbed 'Hairy Mary', an oblique reference to what remained of her black mane and surprisingly hairy armpits. Her face had been burnt beyond recognition and personal items which would have given some clues had been utterly destroyed by the flames. Also, her handbag was missing. One could assume the terrified woman had bolted in panic entombing herself in the lavatory cubicle under the impression that she would be safe. In fact the smoke and fumes had killed her, the final immolation occurring later, the inferno taking swift control despite the firefighters' efforts.

Tom Culley shuffled the bleak photographs of the corpse and wondered what the artist's impression of a reconstructed face would turn up. The only thing he *was* sure of was that this Jane Doe was connected with Abigail Griffith. Why else would the person who had forged Griffith's signature in Wiffin's book stand aside? It wasn't as if using a false name at a stupid preview sale was any sort of crime.

St Clair's little gobbet of information about Griffith's love-in with a government VIP was intriguing. But clearly Hairy Mary was never the frontbencher he alluded to. For a start even a rough guess at the dead woman's appearance tallied with no-one he had ever seen in the news and, in any event, any high-profile politician would be missed in hours as the security surrounding such people was red hot. But if the girl killed in the fire was not the mysterious minister, could she fit into the equation from another angle?

Culley's reasoning slid aside from the photographs spread out on his desk and he contemplated the mystery obliquely. Maybe he was trying to force a square peg into a round hole here. Maybe the Griffith connection had nothing whatsoever to do with the Zelini business. Trying to tag his anonymous cadaver with Griffith was all bollocks. Perhaps the case he *should* be investigating was the Griffith murder? If, despite Superintendent Ackroyd's best efforts, no informer had come up with any names of villains who turned over the Hampstead place, what if Griffith had another source of income? What if the apparently lawful art editor had been supplementing her bank balance with a little blackmail? St Clair had been pretty excited about his scoop. Whoa! A junior minister of the Crown shacked up in a lesbian relationship. Pity he was adamant that he would deny such knowledge if Culley tried to make him swear to it – presumably he had plans to exploit the story himself at the right moment or pass it under the table for a cash payout. He said he had photographic evidence, though snapshots of two women on a terrace couldn't prove anything. Back-up evidence would be necessary even for a tabloid exposé: receipts, independent witnesses to a regular relationship at the very least. But perhaps St Clair had already covered that – after all he was an experienced journalist and not a man to take fright easily. Trouble was the press was awash with ready cash for this sort of sleaze if it could be proven, though messing with a politician could not only be dangerous but lay open any publication to expensive litigation.

But what if Griffith had no such qualms? Supposing Abigail Griffith had some documentation – a video, letters even? Evidence she could use to extract money from this alleged lover? As St Clair remarked, lesbian relationships in public life were yet to be accepted by the vast majority of the voters. Having proof of such an affair would give Abigail Griffith enormous power. Supposing, in desperation, this important ladyfriend of hers decided to employ some heavies to retrieve the evidence, an undercover operation which went over the top? Or did it? Culley's imagination fizzed with the possibilities of even government agents being moved in to save the minister's reputation? After all, one more scandal of this sort could surely ditch any hopes of re-election. Were the stakes high enough to merit eliminating Abigail Griffith or had he just seen too many American conspiracy movies?

Culley lit a cigarette, mulling over the dangerous turn his

digging into what amounted to little more than a missing person inquiry had taken.

It wasn't as if the fire had been deliberately set. Arson was not on the cards. No point. One surprising spin-off from the case had been the fact that the house Madame Zelini rented from her sleeping partner had been under-insured, certainly not sufficient to cover the loss of a valuable property in a prime location. Having discovered the financial involvement of Turner Developments, Culley's surprise at the low value that had been put on the premises was considerable. Raymond Turner was certainly no fool – perhaps one of his minions had got it wrong, in which case, according to the gossip in the business papers, his boss would spill blood on the carpet in bucketfuls.

Getting professionally involved with Tiziana Zelini at all seemed a dodgy investment. Culley's questions about the fashion house put to his financial press buddies gave little room for doubt that the woman's status as a top-flight designer had been plummeting over several seasons, the backing of a speculative wizard such as Raymond Turner sure to go pear-shaped if the balance sheets continued to veer into the red.

Kline erupted into the general office, breaking into Culley's reverie like a gunshot. He glared round the crowded room, counting heads.

"Isn't it about time you got off your arse, Culley, and sorted out Hairy Mary's sugar daddy?" He threw down close-up shots of the jewelled heart the dead girl had been wearing, the only item relatively unscathed in the fire. Culley leapt up, scattering papers on to the floor, aware of suppressed giggles from WPC Teller.

"My next job, sir. Problem is Bond Street's pretty quiet on Sundays."

Kline swore under his breath, realising too late he had stepped right in it with this Smart Alec. Trouble was Kline had lost touch with the time sheets, the urgent need to close down this Zelini farce riding roughshod over any notion of weekends. He turned on his heel, making sure he had the last word before slamming out of the building.

"He's right, Tom," Wendy Teller put in. "Tracing who bought a pricy item like that shouldn't be difficult. Those diamond hearts are the latest fashion craze, all the rage over the last couple of years, but I'm told the one Hairy Mary had was worth a fortune. Cuts down the outlets considerably. Would you like me to help out? I could take some photos round to the Fulham Road designers and you could tackle the Bond Street end."

Culley looked morose, knowing he'd missed a trick here, worse still having it pointed out by Kline in front of a full house. He dragged his attention back to Wendy Teller and struggled to laugh it off. They agreed to share the legwork as she suggested, Wendy brimming with enthusiasm, keen to have a role to play in the Zelini case.

The arrival of Matt Randall at La Colomba lightened the atmosphere considerably. Being Canadian he bridged an invisible gap between the American and the English faction and his genuine good nature made him just about the perfect house guest.

He was charming to the ladies in an unthreatening way, his clean-cut looks refreshingly different from the average hanger-on Philip Barclayson invited to stay. Matt's grasp of the academic discussions on art history seemed sparse but his jokey manner won them all over, even Royd-Chiddingstone, a dry stick if ever there was one.

Anabel took to him immediately, relaxing in the diminution of serious debate, which had previously dominated the dinner table causing Rocky Minola's eyes to glaze over and, once, lulling Prince Felix to nod off completely. Matt's wardrobe was even more meagre that Anabel's, his daytime gear comprising chinos, a sweatshirt and desert boots and his evening attire, in contrast to the older men's formal wear, merely a fresh shirt under a bottle green corduroy suit distinctly thinning at the knees and elbows.

Unlike the recently departed Freddie Knight, Matt was financially independent and almost up to scratch academically, which allowed Alys to let him float free through her mixed bag of friends. Rocky Minola and her princeling were enchanted and even Royd-Chiddingstone gave his thumbs up before jetting off to Paris before his anticipated rejoining of the house party when it reassembled at Rocky's palazzo in Venice.

Matt politely refused the invitation to join the Minola party, insisting he had more than enough research to catch up on in Philip's library. That afternoon, as they sat on the shady side of the terrace enjoying mint juleps after lunch, the talk drifted smoothly away from Rocky's disappointed response to the denied abduction of Philip's young man for the remainder of her holiday in Italy.

"Alys and I will keep each other company," he cheerfully insisted. "And by the time you get back Anabel and I will astound you by our professional application."

Amid polite titters Anabel managed to explain that she too was decamping to Venice the following week. "Alys is letting me borrow her flat. I can hardly wait to explore Venice for the first time."

"Really? You've never swooned to the delights of La Serenissima?" He looked astonished.

Anabel passed a hand through her curls, feeling herself to be the focus of several pairs of eyes, thankful for the Valentino sunglasses Alys had pressed upon her, a gift, just one of the thoughtful touches the woman instinctively produced.

"In that case," Matt continued, "you must excuse me if I monopolise Anabel until you leave."

"She could do with some company apart from us old fogeys," James gallantly put in. "Show her the delights of Lucca, dear boy. Seize the moment!"

Anabel was taken aback by Mr Royd-Chiddingstone's unexpected outburst, a man not given to romantic effusions and the one guest who Anabel suspected was harbouring reservations regarding her business relationship with their host.

Next morning, true to his word, Matt insisted on driving her into Lucca in his hire car, a jolly little runabout which bounced over the rutted lanes like a pram on 'speed'.

Once in the lovely little town, they settled for coffee in the square, the statue of Puccini seemingly approving of all the young lovers enjoying the April sunshine. Getting to know Matt Randall was like sliding down a snow slope on a tin tray. Fun. Exhilarating. He was an easy companion, seamlessly extracting Anabel's fears and expectations of her month in Tuscany under Philip Barclayson's sponsorship. Naturally there were aspects of her dealings with the old fox which remained secret and at the back of her mind Anabel was well aware that a 'researcher' was just another busybody. An undercover investigative journalist even?

"Let's go see some churches," he said with a grin, pulling her from her seat and taking her arm to lead her into San Frediano's.

Anabel laughed, tying up her hair in Kim's Hermes scarf. "Isn't that a bit touristy?"

"But of course! But it's what you *do* in Italy, angel. Today we are *en fête*. This is no grey Monday morning in London and we are not on a working holiday. You and I, Anabel Gordon, are going to 'do the sights'."

The interior of the huge church struck a chill after the warmth outside, the dimness glittering with candles, the vaulted ceiling echoing with the footfalls of the few holidaymakers. Matt wandered off to investigate a painting in a side chapel, leaving Anabel to stroll from the nave and pass through to another side chapel, a space barely lit and eerily silent. Incense hung on the air like a drug. Anabel relaxed, glad to be alone at last, exhausted by the continuous demands at La Colomba. She padded towards the altar intrigued by a glass showcase dominating it. It was only as she got close that it hit her.

The showcase was in fact a reliquary containing the incorruptible body of a saint, the limbs and features desiccated and black but perfectly preserved, the cadaver lovingly dressed in white with veil and flowers in her hair like a bride. It had a savage beauty, a mesmerising presence too powerful to ignore. Anabel's heart thumped painfully in her chest, her breath ragged with shock.

She felt herself fainting and just as she was about to fall Matt appeared out of the darkness, grabbing her in his arms. He eased her into a seat outside the chapel and begged a glass of water from the attendant selling booklets at the door.

At last she felt able to go back out into the sunshine, grasping his arm as if her life depended on it, her face ashen.

"Anabel, whatever happened in there? You look as if you'd seen a ghost."

She slumped down on the stone steps, feeling nauseous. "It was the shock. I hadn't realised . . . That body laid on the altar. So lifelike. It reminded me . . ."

"Reminded you?"

"I only saw it in the paper yesterday. A friend . . . She died last week just after I left. Beaten to death in her own flat. By burglars."

"That mugging in Hampstead? She was a pal of yours? Really? Jeepers!"

Anabel nodded. "I ought to go back for the funeral. She had no-one else you see. No family. I should telephone someone . . ." She faltered, still confused. The shock of seeing the holy relic displayed on the altar had finally brought it home to her. Abigail Griffith was at this moment lying in her shroud on a mortuary slab. Gee-Gee had been murdered.

"I'll drive us back. Don't fly home, Anabel. We've hardly had a chance to get to know each other. And you can hardly help your friend by breaking off your work for a funeral, can you?"

Twelve

Anabel fell in love with Venice. Despite the rain. Despite the exorbitant prices. Despite the pigeons. Philip turfed her out of the car in Verona where he was dining with a former student, insisting that her first glimpse of Venice must be from across the water. Rocco organised her passage with a party of Japanese tourists, handing her and her hand luggage to the courier with eye-balling intensity, rattling away in brusque Italian, presumably threats ensuring her safe delivery to the door of Alys's little flat.

Philip had been absolutely right. The splendour of the city slowly emerging from the mist over the lagoon sent a quiver of excitement right through to her bones. On the quayside the courier passed her to a surly colleague awaiting the arrival of the travel group and after an exchange of a bundle of notes and a wordless appraisal of the skinny bird of passage, he weaved his way through a maze of narrow lanes eventually to deposit her at her temporary perch. Nervously, Anabel thrust more notes into his hand, grinning away, glowing with an unquenchable delight at this unexpected turn of events.

The address to which she had been sent was a house closely shuttered, the bleak exterior oppressively aloof. Unlocking the dingy door off the *calle* and climbing the dark stairs to second-floor level, the silence of the empty house was unnerving. Alys had warned that many residents preferred to live in Maestre, the mainland industrial complex, either leaving their Venetian property unoccupied or, in the high season, letting it to foreign visitors.

In fact, once she had fumbled her way across the darkened hallway to fling open the shutters, Alys's pied-à-terre proved rather more than she had been led to expect, the high ceilings dappled with intermittent sunshine, the closeted rooms scented with bowls of lavender.

Anabel practically swooned with pleasure – the place was so 'right'. A bedroom led off a living room toplit by a fanlight and, set apart along a tiled passage, a tiny kitchen and bathroom commanded a rear view of a mossy yard with terracotta pots, enclosed by the backs of houses in the next alley. Almost within reach, the closest boasted a rusty balcony on which a parrot sat hunched in its cage below a billowing line of washing stretched between the two adjacent buildings.

Rocco arrived within the hour, toting the heavy luggage and all her painting gear. He was obviously familiar with Alys's bolthole and explained the temperamental quirks of the gas stove and geyser. He sprawled on one of the velvet sofas downing a beer he had found in the fridge, obligingly sketching a rough map of the vicinity and describing the route she should take to reach the Minola palazzo for her morning conference with Philip.

This reference to the real reason for her visit struck the first chill note in what to Anabel stretched ahead like a magical mystery tour. There was work to be done. She poured herself a glass of wine and quickly changed the subject, quizzing Rocco on the variety of duties Philip's minder undertook. Twilight imperceptibly dimmed the room and Anabel became aware of the clatter of people passing on the little street below, the rhythmic echo of hundreds of feet pounding the stone setts, people noisily intent on the next thing. Voices blurred into laughter, children shouted, dogs barked. Soon the silent, curiously menacing atmosphere of the deserted *calle* had been transformed. Anabel relaxed, feeling safe in the crowd again.

After Rocco had sloped off, she unpacked her satchel and set up a pin board on the easel, arranging an assortment of photographs and art reproductions torn from magazines in a random collage. She stood back, eyeing the collection with growing interest. All pictures of little girls of nine or ten years of age dressed in nineteenth-century frills, eyes wide with apprehension. Perhaps Philip's current commission might be interesting after all. She sat down and made some rapid sketches, forgetting to eat, absorbed in this new challenge.

In contrast, Tom Culley's investigation had struck a sour note. Neither he nor WPC Wendy Teller had had any luck tracing the retailer of the dead woman's ruby and diamond heart. Many jewellers were openly dismissive, several insisting that identifying such work would be impossible without having the piece itself open to scrutiny, photographs being of no use whatsoever. Kline was reluctant to allow the evidence off the premises without at least a hint that an identification was on the cards and he was certainly not putting the valuable piece in the hands of a female officer. No way.

Culley lumbered on, insinuating himself into cramped workrooms in Hatton Garden and expensive showrooms in Bond Street, all to no effect. Interest flagged. He decided to return to his original hunch and check out the Abigail Griffith connection.

He arrived unannounced at the *Eve Now* offices and tried to get in to see St Clair.

"In conference," his tight-lipped PA snapped, determined to make no further concessions to the police. Culley's buttonholing of Ackroyd's sergeant, Mike Lee, had satisfied him that the A Team in the Abigail Griffith murder inquiry had got nothing more, in fact considerably less, out of St Clair than he had himself. Either Griffith's managing editor had clammed up on the VIP lesbian liaison St Clair had stumbled upon or Lee was being economical with the data. Culley put his money on St Clair having second thoughts on his initial loose-lipped discussion with Culley, having yet to decide how to handle this tasty morsel of information. However, the fact remained that the Zelini corpse was no government minister and, as Kline strove to impress on his crew, the identification of Hairy Mary was the *only* case they were investigating, the Griffith angle being well off limits.

Then Culley went to see Mavis Thompson. But Mavis Thompson had gone. There was a new secretary, pert in that slick style of city girls on the way up, which Culley recalled all too clearly from his dealing room days.

"Miss Thompson's taking time out. Said she wanted to consider her future. May take early retirement," she added, turning back to her console with a flick of the tawny bob which to Culley's recollection was the last tint his ex-girlfriend Gerry had favoured. It must go with the vibes.

He stood his ground and insisted on seeing Griffith's replacement, the new art editor. Miss Fixit demurred, rattling out a well-versed put-down featuring key phrases like 'deadline', 'editorial meeting' and 'tight schedule'. Hearing raised voices in the outer office, the editor's door burst open, a tall bloke in black leathers filling the entry.

"What's up, Daisy?"

"More police."

"Christ Almighty! Give us a break. We're trying to get some work done here."

Culley flashed his ID and after a further irascible exchange both men moved into Abigail's office. In fact, Tom had not planned to dip into this particular murky pool, but what the hell.

Griffith's replacement introduced himself, confidently slouching behind the massive desk.

'Craig Sellick. I got shoved in here from AGM's boys' mag upstairs. Oh yeah, we were all cut up at losing Griffith like that," he put in as a polite afterthought, tipping back his chair to balance his biker's boots on a chair piled high with proofs.

"I was wondering about Ms Griffith's personal papers. Office diary? Private correspondence? Photographs?"

"Your colleague went through all that when he was here."

"Sergeant Lee?"

"Whatever . . . He found nothing interesting. We boxed everything up and sent it down to Filing. Do you need it after all? Second thoughts?" he added with a curl of the lip, obviously a member of the public unaware of the latest police-friendly publicity handouts.

"If your secretary would oblige? Thank you, sir. Actually, Mr Sellick, I hoped to speak with Miss Thompson."

"Gone. Sick leave or something. I got shanghaied for this job like I said and naturally prefer to use my own staff. People used to my funny little ways. We offered Miss T. another job downstairs but she's been here a long time. These old biddies get sniffy. Don't like new methods, know what I mean?"

"Upsetting to lose her job on top of everything else. Still in shock no doubt."

"In shock?"

"Miss Thompson found the body."

Sellick stiffened. "Oh yeah. Nasty business."

After more desultory conversation, Culley withdrew, following Mavis Thompson's stand-in down to the Filing Department to retrieve the private papers ejected from the dead woman's desk. He glanced at his watch. It was nearly six and, with nothing else to fill his timesheet, Tom decided to drive out to Chiswick and commiserate with Mavis Thompson for whom he felt a certain empathy, each of them fumbling to find a toehold in the rockfall the death of Abigail Griffith had brought about.

The sister opened the door, cooking smells drifting deliciously through the maisonette. She recognised Culley immediately and, hearing his voice, Mavis hurried into the hall, her glasses in her hand, eyes narrowed against the glare of the security spotlight focussing on the man outside the front door.

"Oh, Sergeant, do come in. How nice to see you," she said, insisting he joined them for a sherry. Mavis had discarded her office uniform, her drawstring trousers and sloppy sweater lending an informal touch which encouraged Culley to drop the official tone. They settled in the sitting room in front of the gas fire, the sister bustling about in a mumsy way, then quickly excusing herself to attend to the supper. Culley jumped in with both feet, taking his chance on this one-to-one with Griffith's closest colleague, the two women boxed up in the same office for years surely exchanging *some* confidences.

He described his conversation with Craig Sellick and admitted that the investigation was at a standstill.

"I did not wish to stay on after Gee-Gee's death. Feelings were too raw. In any event being downgraded to what amounted to a typing pool at my stage in life would have been unendurable."

"You've retired."

"For the present. I may join a friend in a month or two. She has her own employment agency. Mollie's been urging me to go into partnership for some time."

"Very nice too." Culley paused, phrasing his next assault with care. "I know this must be very painful for you, Miss Thompson, but if we are to solve this murder we have to explore every aspect of Ms Griffith's private life. There is also the identification of the woman who died in the Zelini fire to consider. The only connection between these two investigations is your late employer. The person who was killed in the fire is, in all probability, the woman to whom Ms Griffith passed her invitation and who subsequently forged her signature. Are you sure you have no idea who this was? There is a rumour that Ms Griffith had special friends, close relationships with other women if you understand me . . . ?"

Behind the thick lenses her eyes glittered. "Lesbianism is sometimes considered a dirty word, Sergeant, but please, do not hesitate to use it on my account. I assure you Gee-Gee's affections were given only outside the office. You do not embarrass me. We were all aware of her leanings but there was absolutely no problem at work. We girls were perfectly comfortable working with her. Gee-Gee was the best boss one could wish for."

Culley tensed, hoping he had not flatfooted it all over the lady's sensitivities, Mavis Thompson being, in the last resort, his only lead. He stayed silent, hearing the sister banging away in the kitchen, waiting to see which way the wind blew with Griffith's PA.

"There was one girl," she said at last, moving to snatch up a newspaper lying on the coffee table. She impatiently turned pages, frowning with concentration and then, with a little cry of triumph, folding the paper at the fashion pages and handing it to Culley.

He placed his sherry glass on a small side table before taking the paper from her.

"See this model in the cashmere sweater?" she said.

"The one with the frizzy hair?"

"Yes. Well, there was a contributor Gee-Gee used when she could. An artist. Used to do line drawings for us occasionally. Illustrations. She looked rather like this girl in the paper. It struck me this morning as soon as I saw it. Almost identical."

"Her name?"

"Gordon. Miss Gordon. I think Gee-Gee called her Annie."

"You think she may have given this girl her invitation?"

"If she ever had one! I couldn't swear to it. I have – had! – a typist who opened the post. But if the magazine sent someone to represent them at this designer sale there are only a few at the office who would be interested and you've already eliminated them from your inquiries, I'm sure."

Culley nodded, staring at the knitwear feature with all the intensity of a fashion victim. "May I take this, Miss Thompson? Just this page? You do know this woman's address, I take it?"

"No. I'm afraid not. But it's probably among those papers boxed up for you by the Filing Department. Gee-Gee's contacts."

He rose, anxious to be alone with his Pandora's box, clutching at straws in this bloody case. In fact, parked in a convenient lay-by, it took less than twenty minutes to sift Anabel Gordon's address from the stack of paperwork. Impatient to check her out he drove straight over to the Adelphi Grill, catching Dimitri as he was about to close up behind his last customer of the night.

"Gone, mate. Ain't seen her lately."

"A forwarding address?"

Dimitri shrugged, his sad smile expressive.

"When did you last see her exactly?"

He hazarded a date off the top of his head, vague as ever, never anxious to fill in details for the police about his dubious clientele let alone his dodgy lodger who'd even had her phone cut off.

Culley drove home on air. The date the Greek said he last saw his fuzzy-haired tenant was the morning of the fire. At last, from sheer brutal persistence, he'd cracked the mystery of the unnamed corpse clogging up Kline's crime sheets. Now, maybe, they'd let him in on the other half of the mystery: who killed Griffith?

Thirteen

Next morning Culley burst into Kline's office with barely
a by-your-leave, grinning like a fool, flinging Mavis
Thompson's newspaper down on the Chief Inspector's desk
with a flourish. Kline looked up from his letters with a
surprisingly mild response.

"Gone into the frock business, Sergeant? In-depth investigation like they taught you at Hendon?"

"This model in the pink jumper is a dead ringer for Hairy
Mary, sir."

"Who says?"

"Griffith's secretary."

"Knows for a fact who the invite was passed on to, does
she? One of Griffith's lezzies?"

"You knew about that?"

"So what else is new?"

Culley smoothed his tie, suddenly aware that this supposed
identification was, in official terms, horribly thin. He repeated
Mavis Thompson's suggestion, throwing in Georghiou's con-
firmation that his lodger had not been seen since the night of
the fire.

"Greek cafe owner. In Brixton, you say. Any form?"

Culley stiffened. Kline was in a funny mood. Smooth.
Chirpy. Like he had an ace up his sleeve.

"Not that I know of, sir. Seemed OK to me."

"Really? Well, cop this lot, Culley. That WPC you put on the road has come up with a winner. Found some chi-chi designer boutique off the Brompton Road. Owner thought he recognised the necklace."

"The diamond heart?"

"What other fucking crown jewels we got stashed away then?"

"From photographs? The jeweller recognised it just from Teller's photographs?"

"I sent her back with Fraser so the man could clock the real item. No mistake. Apparently in 1977 the trade found out stuff hallmarked with a special jubilee mark doubled sales. They're hoping to do the same with a millennium mark. This year the mark's a 'Z' and because the millennium mark is likely to be in huge demand very few 'Z' pieces are being issued. They're holding out for the big one. This locket item is a 'Z' and when Teller's jeweller checked his books he confirmed it was a special order for a Sheikh Hassan. Paid for in cash in time for St Valentine's day."

"So we know who bought it. But who was it for? Was it delivered? Gift wrapped?"

"Jeweller won't say. Obviously too good a customer to compromise. But I reckon he gave this sheikh the tip-off. The buyer's shot back to the Middle East under cover of diplomatic immunity."

Culley sagged. "We can check it from this end, sir. Now I've got a name to go on we can put out a search. Check out Hassan's background – see if he has any links with the Gordon woman."

"Then what?"

"If we can't question the sheikh and we can't locate the girl that only leaves the dental records. Compare them with the corpse."

Kline sighed. "Look, I don't want to rub these diplomatic people up the wrong way for nothing. You know how touchy they can be. Find out more about the woman. Lives over a greasy spoon you say. Doesn't sound like Hairy Mary. Our burnt offering was expensively maintained, manicured and wearing the charred remnants of a couture suit. How could a skint illustrator for women's magazines *afford* Zelini stuff? Even in a sale. Get real, Culley."

"She must have been doing favours on the side. Even a one-night stand with one of those sheikhs would be big numbers. My girlfriend once went to a Saudi prince's house for dinner and all the women were discreetly told to place their evening bags on a salver. When they got them back, every purse had a nice little item tucked inside."

"Sounds like my kids' birthday parties," Kline laughed. "What did your girlfriend pick up?"

"A gold pendant. Never wore it. Not her style she said. But as I say—"

"Enough chit-chat, Culley. Just get back out there and nail down some facts. I don't want any cock-ups on this one. I've had enough flak from Ackroyd as it is."

"Any chance of me being seconded to the Griffith case, sir? On a temporary basis, of course."

"Just bugger off, Culley, and check your information. For all we know this Gordon woman's just gone off to Ibiza for a knees-up. Get a search warrant for her flat. See what you can nose out before we start shouting."

Meanwhile, in Venice, Culley's 'corpse' was living in style, Philip Barclayson's flavour of the month, work moving along like a steam train. Less than a week after moving into Alys's flat she had finished the groundwork on the new portrait, a much smaller production than 'Cicely Alexander' but with the same swirling brushstrokes. Another fair-haired moppet but this time all togged up in a cape and floppy beret, her eyes sliding slyly to face the world, a knowing child compared with Cicely.

In a mood of tieing up loose ends she even managed to leave yet another message on Kimberley Carter's mobile quoting Alys's telephone number in the Venice apartment, feeling quite proud of her efforts to come clean with the Twiggy doppelgänger.

Rocky Minola had invited Philip and his friends to join her at a private view at a new gallery set up by a Texan dealer in a street conveniently situated close to Harry's Bar. Philip insisted he escort Anabel, and anxious to foster his good opinion while it lasted Anabel leapt at the chance.

But clothes were a problem – Rocky Minola's soirees had already mopped up Anabel's meagre stock of evening wear. The cut on her thigh had not completely healed and, risking a black chiffon micro skirt teamed with a gold lamé sweater she had picked up from a market stall, the addition of the Zelini velvet cloak not only disguised the scar but added a touch of mystery. Anabel had never worn the cloak since the night of the fire. It had bad vibes, unlike Kimberley Carter's crocodile handbag. She had become inseparable from the wonderful bag, the mere scent of its luxurious lining sending a frisson of pleasure each time she dipped into it.

They all met up for champagne cocktails at Rocky's palazzo before strolling like an overdressed family party through the crowded lanes to the gallery. It seemed that the whole city was intent on an evening promenade, the bands playing on either side of the square blending and then dividing in a sweet cacophony of sound. Rocco brought up the rear, his massive bulk reinforcing the invulnerability of this ill-assorted group.

The gallery, unlike the ones in London Anabel was familiar with, was dark as a tomb, icon-like pictures cunningly lit like jewels in a velvet-lined coffer, the rooms set about with gilded chairs much too ornate to sit upon. Fairy food on lustre platters was passed round, the clientele disappointingly geriatric, a sprinkling of beautiful Italian girls in long silk dresses sparingly distributed. Anabel retained her cape, the voluptuous folds augmenting her high-street mini. She accepted more wine, clinking glasses with a spectacled academic scarecrow who introduced himself as a Cambridge Fellow on sabbatical, intent, it was all too apparent, on claiming the English girl for afters. Catching a glimpse of a familiar figure in the mêlée Anabel made her excuses, surprised and, yes, delighted to spot her old bedmate Solomon Cheyney in deep discussion with the Italian gallery owner himself.

She mingled with the crowd, admiring Solomon's deft manipulation of the paying customers, his smiles interspersed with rapt attention as Rocky's matronly friends eagerly introduced themselves. Anabel had to admit Solomon was good looking, admittedly not as impeccably groomed as the suave Italian men but owning a certain rugged appeal like a man with a five o'clock shadow. At last he saw her and, sliding through the heavily perfumed crush of bodies, grabbed her arm and without so much as a hello, whispered, "Let's vamoose, lady. I need some air."

He sketched a breezy farewell to their host and frogmarched her to a launch tied up at the canalside, shouting instructions in rapid Italian to the man at the wheel and whisking

Anabel off into the dark before she had a chance to utter a single word.

Back on the beat, Culley had to admit his kneejerk reaction to Mavis Thompson's tentative suggestion regarding the girl who might have been the recipient of Griffith's Zelini invitation had been premature.

He showed Wiffin the press cutting but the butler was unconvinced. He tried to track down any friends or family of the Gordon female but hit a brick wall. His search of her flat above the Brixton cafe only seemed to confirm Kline's suspicion that the kid was off on holiday. All make-up and toiletries had been cleared from the bathroom, no suitcases or passport were in evidence and only a few grubby sweaters and a threadbare duffle coat remained in the wardrobe. A woman popping out for the evening to attend a designer sale hardly packs up all her worldly goods beforehand, does she? Even so, the coincidence was uncanny. If Mavis Thompson said Griffith was on more than a professional basis with this artist woman, Culley believed her.

Trouble was the more he tried to pin him down, the vaguer Dimitri Georghiou became. Had his lodger vanished before the fire or after? Did she have an Arab boyfriend? Did men visit her upstairs? Was she likely to own valuable jewellery? Gifts? As the grilling continued the Greek became less and less cooperative, his shrugs more frequent, the likelihood of an accurate statement vaporising in the garlic-laden atmosphere of his steamy kitchen.

Culley decided to try another tack, to hack at the enigma from another angle. He drove over to Turner Development Corporation headquarters in Grosvenor Street and insisted on an interview with Raymond Turner, determined to unravel the financial cat's cradle in which the man had unaccountably involved himself with Madame Zelini and her failing fashion house.

Unlike St Clair, Raymond Turner did not hide behind a phalanx of receptionists and Culley was surprisingly admitted straight off. The big man's private office was workmanlike, large but lacking the glitzy blueprint of his expensive properties, the view blocked by venetian blinds.

Turner, grey haired and bulky, rose politely from behind his desk to wave Culley to a seat, a pale girl with big eyes and an extravagant fall of blond hair perched on a chair at the boss's elbow. She toted no shorthand notebook or sheaf of papers and kept her seat. Whether this ornament was staff or merely decoration was unclear. Turner ignored her presence completely and Culley struggled to keep his attention on the matter in hand. She seemed nervous, fixing Culley with eyes ringed from lack of sleep, her extreme pallor and air of fatigue lending a curious appeal. Culley had never been attracted to waifs before and found her vulnerability disturbing. Turner himself was all affability, pushing aside the files on his desk to listen to Culley's careful questions.

Turner's interest in the fashion business was, he cheerfully admitted, an indulgence. One of many indulgences, which included the financial backing of a few British film makers. "A charity if ever there was one," he laughed.

"I admire Tiziana's work. I shall refloat the whole project as quickly as possible before this tragic accident causes gossip."

"Gossip?"

"I don't have to tell you, sergeant, what a bitchy business the designer game is. One whiff of scandal and suddenly the Zelini tag is tarnished. That is why I need to have this nameless corpse identified without more delay. The longer the mystery hangs over us the more wild the talk. Arson's the least of it. I have to warn you, sergeant, that if the police produce no results in the next few days I shall be forced to employ my own investigators." His tone hardened. "You have no leads at all as yet?"

"Only this." Culley laid the newspaper feature on the desk. "She looked like this. We think her name was Anabel Gordon but we are still attempting to check it out. I've searched her flat in Brixton but everything's gone. Does the name ring a bell?"

The girl beside Turner left the room, putting both men off balance. Turner swiftly regained his composure, scrutinising the press cutting with close attention.

"Anabel Gordon, eh? A.G. And this kid's vanished? You sure? Your forensic people could easily check out the corpse against this girl's medical records. Elementary, my dear Watson." Turner's smile did not reach his eyes.

"We're in the process of pursuing that angle, sir," Culley stiffly replied.

Turner raised a quizzical eyebrow and rose, pushing buttons on his console and curtly inviting someone called Angie to escort the police officer to the door. Culley's time slot had, it was all too apparent, expired.

"Get back to me as soon as you've got some real evidence, sergeant. Naturally I am always at your disposal if I can offer any assistance."

Culley found himself out in the car park like a ball kicked into touch, far from certain which side Turner was on. That was the trouble these days: he had lost touch with dealing with big snappers like Raymond Turner. Men like that used small fry like Culley for appetisers and spat them out just as soon as they ceased to be tasty.

But as he drove away he conceded it had not been an entire waste of time. Turner was the sort of entrepreneur who intrigued him. He would have to do a deeper research job to unravel that financial pike's fishing grounds. All that rot about fashion and films being 'little indulgences' cut no ice. Men like Turner never got where they were by indulging themselves. Apart from that gorgeous waif he kept on the side, of course. Culley reckoned he could do with an indulgence like that. The pity was he could no longer afford it.

Fourteen

After whisking her from the gallery Solomon Cheyney led Anabel across tiny bridges and canals until she felt quite dizzy, the destination being a crowded fish restaurant, the cheerful racket of locals out on the town reminding her of Dimitri's caff on a Saturday night.

The Englishman was greeted like the prodigal son, clasped in the embrace of the proprietor, his bonhomie enclosing Cheyney's girl of the moment as if she were the latest of a series of identical girls welded to Solomon's arm.

They were shoehorned into a corner niche, the cloth swiftly replaced, a carafe of wine appearing with a clatter of fresh cutlery and a candle in a bottle. After the initial flurry the service was slow. But they had a lot of filling in to do and the wine and the heady atmosphere of the small *pescatori* wove its magic, the constraints in which Anabel had been trapped ever since the fire evaporating in the smoky air.

"That last time," she ventured, circling the rim of her glass with a tentative finger, "I had no idea you were married."

He laughed. "Me? Married? Whatever gave you that idea?"

"Your little boy – at the flat."

He sobered. "Ah, yes. Freddie. I'd forgotten Freddie had introduced himself. Sorry about that."

"It was quite a shock."

Solomon smiled. "He's a right little passion-killer, that boy. You should have stayed for breakfast and got to know each other. Freddie stays with me most weekends. His mother's something of a lush, has to dry out from time to time. We never married." He lit a cigarette, eyeing Anabel with the attention he normally only gave to pictures brought to his gallery. "Freddie's the only good thing came out of that relationship. Great little guy."

Anabel sipped her wine, warming to this new man who, with no effort at all, made her feel at ease.

"Now tell me why you're here," he said.

At that moment the food arrived: a platter of *gran fritto misto* garnished with lemon slices, fennel and salad, the aroma of the deep fried bits of sole, eel, squid and scampi rising like the very essence of the sea. Her eyes widened. She grinned at Solomon and heaped his plate, realising that for the first time since that terrible last visit to Ronnie's flat in Kings Cross she was ravenous.

He walked her back to Alys's apartment and after a moment's hesitation she invited him in. The house echoing with their footsteps seemed as unwelcoming as ever, the stillness of the vacant rooms spooky after the noisy restaurant and lanes still crowded with late-night revellers. That was the odd thing about this city, she decided. One moment all bustle and warmth, the next dank and silent as if the ancient stones of the submerged foundations were, inch by inch, seeping up eventually to drown any residents brave enough to tough it out. Somewhere two cats started wailing, the unearthly sounds as gut-wrenching as the strangled cry of a vixen.

Inside, she threw the Zelini cloak in the corner and with all the lamps lit and a pot of coffee steaming, Anabel's mood lightened. Under Solomon's persistent questioning she found herself confessing her misgivings about her latest commission from Philip Barclayson. With a strict promise of secrecy she showed him the half-finished portrait.

"Whistler," he breathed, closing in on the sloe-eyed child in the sketchy cape, the rounded features almost complete, the air of Lolita-like knowingness emanating from the picture in timeless allure.

"It's supposed to be Annie Haden, his niece."

"But not a copy."

"No. But there are lots of sketches in existence and Whistler painted her with his sister of course."

"This was Philip's idea?"

"Oh yes. I finished a full-sized copy of Cicely Alexander and brought it out for him. You know, the Tate exhibit."

She poured the coffee, setting a balloon glass of brandy at his elbow.

"You signed it?"

"Yes. Just my initials. A.G. I only use my full name for my original work. Obviously nothing to cause any confusion – the Whistler picture's so well known."

Solomon lit a cigarette, eyeing her with amusement. "You do realise, my darling, that the initials thing is a little paranoid? I've noticed this little quirk of yours before – sometimes you even refer to yourself by your initials as if there's a shadow personality lurking in there who comes in useful when you don't wish to admit to yourself things are not entirely kosher."

She tensed, not sure if he was teasing. She decided to laugh it off, putting aside this disturbing observation of his, realising that in fact it was true. Why else would she have worded that note to Kimberley at the show flat as if A.G. was another person entirely?

"You're being ultra perceptive all of a sudden. Anyway, it's not true," she insisted. "It's just a convenience . . ."

Solomon let it go, grinning to himself. "Well, who's it for, this latest masterpiece of yours?"

Anabel shrugged. "Search me. Philip has a client who's apparently besotted with little girls. Someone in Luxembourg he said."

"Obviously a pervert. A man who likes to drool over children in frills."

"Rubbish! Everyone adores Whistler's portraits. I loved Cicely myself. It turned out really well, Solomon, much the best I've done. Anyway, Philip's not like that. His friend Royd-Chiddingstone agreed I'd done a super job on some water-colours I bought over. He wants me to do some Whistlerish pen and ink drawings of Venice while I'm here." She said nothing about the etchings which were, in anybody's book, a straight knock-off.

"On old parchment paper using special ink Philip provides," Solomon muttered. "Does it never occur to you, my darling, that you're swimming in very dangerous waters here? As I see it Barclayson sells your bona fide copy of the Alexander kid to his client to whet his appetite. A year or so later he contacts this old lecher and says he's come across an unknown Whistler, a ravishing oil sketch of the artist's niece. By then the old fox has knocked up some provenance and—"

"Philip's not really a dealer!"

"Bollocks! He's old, sweetheart. Worrying about his pension not to mention keeping up appearances with that woman he lives with. To someone with Barclayson's connections, drumming up some mythical hoarder who's been keeping your Annie Haden in the attic's child's play. The porn addict in Luxembourg jumps at the chance to nab this real treasure before it comes on the market even if Barclayson feeds him some spiel about it being hot – part of a private collection stolen by the Nazis during the war say, insisting the buyer keeps it for private consumption which is, after all, what an eyeballer for pre-pubescent girlies would want to do anyway. Hey presto. With practically no risk at all Barclayson's copped a bundle and no-one ever catches sight of your fake ever again."

"Philip has an international reputation. He's not a crook."

"Faking is crooked whichever way you dress it up."

"But Annie Haden's an original work," she retorted. "And so are the pen and ink sketches. What's wrong with that?"

Solomon peered into his coffee cup like a fortune teller searching for tea leaves. "It's not what *you* do, it's what these other so-called gentlemen do afterwards. Why does Barclayson provide you with an authentic nineteenth-century canvas, set you up with all the kosher materials? Don't kid me it's never crossed your mind that taking all this trouble to reproduce the brush strokes, using the same subjects and the right gear of an artist long-dead is a con? At best a con? At worst a blot on the poor devil's reputation. Why Whistler, for God's sake? Why not choose a really tripy painter to rip off?"

Anabel snapped. Solomon had gone too far. Baiting her about her copying work had flicked her on the raw and what did he know? Had he ever been in a trap like herself, forced to undertake dubious commissions, forced to let his own work go down the drain? Cheeks flaring, she leapt up and swore, the ugly words resounding in the high-ceilinged room like the tirade of an Italian fishwife.

Solomon fell back, laughing, and made a grab at her as she dodged aside, the two of them tumbling about the floor, her anger dissipating as a growing desire flared between them. He pinned her to the rug, the sexual temperature rising, his weight pressing down on her in mock triumph.

"Give up?" he said, squeezing her thigh.

She yelped in pain, clutching her leg, suddenly aware of the injury the Harley Street doctor had so neatly stitched.

"Christ! Anabel, what have I done?"

She pushed him off, rolling down her stocking, peering at the livid scar. Satisfied, she looked up, affectionately cuffing him as he tried to get a closer look.

"That'll cost you! I've only just got that cut expensively cobbled together. I'll have to have another word with my lawyer," she said, giggling.

He swigged the dregs of brandy, raking through his hair, utterly confused, glad that at least she seemed to have forgotten his attack on her work, her outburst of temper doused by the scuffle.

"It's OK," she said, pulling him to his feet. "Come to bed and I'll tell you what really happened." She told him all about the evening of the fire.

Alys's bed was wide and soft as a cloud, and this time Anabel assured herself there would be no small boy climbing aboard.

But in fact, the phone rang, and this time the darkness caught them both disorientated, Anabel flailing about the bedside table in an effort to switch on the light and locate the jangling instrument. It was four a.m.

"Hello? Miss Gordon?" The voice was husky, barely a whisper but in seconds the message was clear. "It's Kim. I've been trying to reach you all evening."

"I'm in Venice."

"I know. I really need all my stuff, Annie. Could you

103

fly back to London? Bring it with you? I don't want it posted."

"Obviously not! You must be bloody barmy, Kimberley Carter. Why should I go to all that trouble when you've already stood me up *twice!*"

"That was unavoidable. I'm being watched. You've no idea what I've been through. I'd come over myself but you've still got my passport."

"Two passports," Anabel snapped. "Do you run them up yourself with your John Bull printing set?"

"I can explain that. But you will come?"

"No, I won't. The passports and everything are in a package I mailed to myself from the airport when you didn't show up. Call at the Adelphi Grill near Brixton market and ask for Dimitri. He'll give it to you."

"You sure? You trust this bloke?"

"Dimitri's my landlord – I'll give him a buzz, say you're coming to collect a parcel for me. No problem."

The audible sigh at the end of the line was like the expiration of a nun in ecstasy. Solomon regarded her from his pillow with eyes like gimlets. Seeing the funny side of all this Anabel had a mental picture of Kimberley Carter laid out on the altar like poor Saint Zita in San Frediano's chapel, a new style vestal virgin.

"Listen," she said, stifling giggles. "I took the loose change from your bag, Kim – I needed it for expenses. OK?"

"Sure. Sorry about all this, Anabel. One of these days I'll tell you all about it but don't try to ring me again and *never* send any more notes."

"Notes?"

"You left a message at the show flat and my boss got hold of it. He thinks you're blackmailing me."

"Me?" she squeaked.

"Just forget you ever saw me, Anabel. And if the police ever find you, roll over and play dead."

"The police?"

"They searched your flat."

"Looking for your passports?"

"I don't know."

The line cut and Anabel fell back on the pillows with a knot of real anxiety gnawing away at her innards. Solomon moved closer, nuzzling her ear. "And what was all that about?" he said.

"Nothing important. Now where were we?"

Fifteen

Tom Culley tried tracking down Anabel Gordon's clientele. He phoned a girl who worked on the *Museums' Technological Monitor*, a specialist publication mainly of interest to art restorers and museum buffs. Asking Marianne Butler to lunch was beyond the call of duty and certainly beyond his expenses sheet in this investigation but he needed to stay in the centre of town. His car was being serviced which forced him on to public transport – a frustrating blip to the day.

Marianne had been a date before he got dazzled by Geraldine Scott-Holden. A pity as it turned out. He had been badly burned by Gerry but then Marianne was the sort easily outshone by debby types and, in all honesty, his path had not crossed Marianne's since a chance meeting at a party in Pimilico last Christmas.

Her surprise at Culley's phone call to her office was veiled – the rarity of the sort of man who could fall off the financial ladder but without so much as a whinge start a new career with the Met was a powerful aphrodisiac.

They met at a Soho bistro not far from her office and Culley wasted a good half-hour making up for lost time before coming clean with his questions about copyists. Marianne was good looking, no doubt about it, her sex appeal thinly disguised by a spiky hairdo, no make-up and an ankle-length black skirt. Her charm lay in her cornflower-blue eyes and a sharp intelligence, which swiftly assessed Culley's motives. In fact, it amused her to be suddenly taken up again like this, fished from Culley's little black book when he needed something.

"A copyist you say. Any photos? I've come across most of the really good ones over the past few years. They try to get inside the restoration labs from time to time."

"Looking for tips?"

Marianne shrugged. "Whatever. This Gordon girl sounds familiar. She advertises in some of the journals I seem to remember. I'll do a search if you like, I've a stack of publications in my files."

Culley attacked his pasta with gusto, grinning at his lunch date with renewed enthusiasm. Now he came to think about it, Marianne had been the last one before Gerry. Things might have turned out differently if he'd stuck to girls like Marianne Butler. He dipped into his document case and produced the dog-eared fashion shot Mavis Thompson had thrown into the ring, the model's unsmiling gaze framed by a mass of black hair like a pre-Raphaelite woman, all smouldering fire. Certainly a dark angel in comparison with that pallid waif who had haunted him ever since his interview with Raymond Turner in Grosvenor Street.

Marianne savoured the bouquet of her Cabernet Sauvignon, fingering the press cutting with distaste.

"Ring any bells, Marianne?"

"Vaguely. Trouble is these gypsy types are two a penny at art colleges up and down the country. I'll ask around if you like. They usually hang out at the big galleries, though copying old masters isn't the moneyspinner it was. More cash in the other thing."

"What other thing?"

"Strictly off limits, of course, and let's be clear on this, I've absolutely no reason to think your girl is involved in dodgy practices so don't quote me."

"Cross my heart."

"If you're really good at pastiche work the latest wheeze is to be employed by stately home owners who want their pictures copied, allegedly for security reasons."

"They put the genuine article in the bank vault and exhibit the copy?"

"The paying public can't tell the difference and if there's a break-in the honest aristo admits the con to the insurance people and gets a wigging. Alternatively, the skint bugger has the option of claiming the insurance and selling the original on the quiet to a collector who makes a hobby of creating a secret hoard. It's generally set up by the dealers, often stolen to order, a buyer already in the pipeline."

"What happens when the burglars find out they've been duped?"

"They pass the parcel damn quick before the fake starts to smell. The more often it changes hands the less willing anyone is to blow the whistle."

"The originals never reappear?"

"Oh yes, eventually maybe. Some countries have looser restrictions on the resale of stolen art than we do and the trick is never to get involved with first-class stuff. Minor artists won't set off alarms like masterpieces which can go into limbo for decades passing from vault to vault as collateral. The mafia have been known to use fine art as a useful bargaining tool, a method of laundering drugs money for instance. Are you investigating a fraud, Tom?"

"Much more interesting than that. I have one unidentified

corpse who may or may not be this black-eyed copyist. And another dead body – a friend of Gordon's as it happens and an art editor like yourself – who was murdered within days of the first woman being smothered in a fire."

"Ouch! And you think they're connected? Both women involved in an international art scam?" The cornflower-blue eyes sparkled.

Culley smiled, raising his hand to order fresh coffee. After the waiter had gone he hastened to dampen down Marianne's enthusiasm, steering the conversation back on the rails, asking her about her job on the *Monitor*, stressing his lowly status as a police sergeant since his dealing room days.

They left the bistro, lulled by the wine, swearing to "do this again *very* soon". Culley hugged her as they parted, promising himself a rematch. Perhaps it was time he got in more practice with girls like Marianne: being burnt out in the flare of Gerry's comet-like exit was bad for his testosterone.

Marianne's comments about insurance fraud were interesting but, he decided, of no relevance in the search for Anabel Gordon. He phoned in to the station and spoke to Wendy Teller, who confirmed Kline's claims about the identity of the buyer of the jewelled heart. That was all he needed: a diplomatic cover-up muddying the waters. He decided to go back to basics and have another go at the Zelini staff. He struggled with the shoppers on the Piccadilly line and eventually fetched up at the showroom just as the office staff were on their tea break. He bagged the chief dragon, a Mrs Aynesley-Foster, whose eyebrows rose in twin arcs of black crayon, any vestige of hair follicles having been tweaked out long since.

"I'm extremely busy, Sergeant. We have an inter-season cruisewear collection being shown next week. You have already interviewed the staff exhaustively. The girls really do have nothing more to add."

"But the two missing invitations are still not accounted for, Mrs Aynesley-Foster. And Mr Turner insists I be given every cooperation."

Raymond Turner's name acted like abracadabra, the twin arcs rising to disappear under the raven bangs over her forehead. After a further frigid exchange observed by the two open-mouthed typists, Mrs Aynesley-Foster admitted defeat and shunted Culley into the back office relegated to the Zelini Financial Director, a middle-aged worrier who introduced himself as George Cayster. In fact, George Cayster was a welcome relief from the Aynesley-Foster female, and the anxious little man in the form-fitting black suit was at least someone with whom Culley could speak toe-to-toe.

A girl brought in a tray of tea and he sent for an extra cup, fussing with the Earl Grey like a maiden aunt, breathing heavily, clearly a man with incipient lung problems.

"And how can I help you, Sergeant?"

Culley chased the lemon slice round his cup, wondering how best to phrase this line of questioning.

"Mr Turner is very anxious for us to clear up this case. The mystifying identity of the unfortunate lady killed in the fire is hampering efforts to a major relaunch of the House of Zelini I gather."

"A tragedy. An absolute tragedy," Cayster agreed.

"You are, of course, aware that your efforts to monitor the clients' invitations went awry. We have whittled the missing cards down to two but we seem unable to reconcile Mrs Aynesley-Foster's list with the ladies who actually attended. *All* the relevant till receipts were lost you say?"

"Every one."

"I know that client confidentiality is involved here, Mr Cayster, but in view of the seriousness of this investigation, may I enquire if a Sheikh Hassan settled any accounts with you in the past? That is not his full name, I realise, but it was all my informant was willing to divulge."

"Absolutely not. And I have to tell you that many clients' bills are paid in cash."

"Cheques, you mean."

"No, cash. Even several items from a single collection. Totals amounting to substantial sums. And there is a cross-over from our other commercial interests, of course."

"You have more fashion outlets?"

"A *prêt-à-porter* in Leeds. Another in Milan. Not to mention a hotel in Edinburgh which also trades under the Zelini umbrella."

Culley sighed, fearing deep waters.

"You must be a busy man, Mr Cayster, overseeing such a multiplicity of operations."

"Mr Turner's auditors advise me."

"Is there any truth in the rumour that the Zelini name is not as commercially viable as it was?"

"Not at all. Our customers are few by international standards, of course, but the money flows in, Sergeant, the money keeps coming. Ladies of style think nothing of spending what I might dare to infer equals your yearly salary on a single spring ensemble. You should speak to our chief vendeuse, Madame Eloise. She knows this business inside out."

Culley made a few notes between reluctant sips of the scented tea remaining in his cup and approached the Zelini business administration at a more mundane level.

"One minor thing before I go, Mr Cayster. Your cleaners."

He consulted his notebook. "A Mrs Miller and a Miss Maguire. Only two? That seems modest for such a large establishment."

"The trainees do a lot and Madame Zelini likes to keep the minor running costs in check. Mrs Miller has been with us for many years but Mary Maguire was new."

"They work as a team?"

"No. Mary did the workroom and Mrs Miller is trusted with the offices and showroom. Both women are privy to confidential information and sketches and therefore their references are closely examined."

"Industrial espionage on the fashion runways?" Culley quipped.

"You may jeer, Sergeant, but stealing designs or even toiles is no laughing matter. As it happens we had to let Maguire go after the fire."

"A staff problem?"

"Oh no. But when the house was gutted the workload was halved."

Culley sobered, repeating his serious concern that the question of the Zelini corpse be laid to rest so that they could all get back to business.

"As a matter of form, may I have the addresses of the cleaning women, sir? My constable has been busy on other lines of inquiry, I'm afraid. Not that the cleaning staff are likely to be harbouring any useful information, I'm sure." Culley's awkward laugh sounded hollow, Cayster's disclosure of the complicated financial ramifications of the supposedly small-time designer house overshadowing any concern about the blanks in the staff statements.

He collected his car and was in half a mind to call it a day. But it had, on the whole, been pretty unproductive and a quick run south of the river to track down the two cleaners would at least clear the files.

Mrs Miller was out. His call on Mary Maguire in Streatham seemed to be equally useless when the door was opened by a yob wearing an 'I Love LA' T-shirt who muttered, "Mum's down the bingo."

"When will she be back?"

The youth moved to shut the door but Culley jammed his foot in it.

"Who wants to know?"

"The police."

The piggy eyes widened. "Try tomorrow night. She's at work till four."

"New job?"

"Yeah. Swanky shop in Mayfair. Candida's Couture," he sneered.

"Good for her. Tell your mum I'll be round tomorrow at five and if she's not in I'll have to take my big boots round to Candida's, won't I?"

"She won't wear that. She's just got the sack from her other job."

"Zelini's?"

"No, Mrs Sagga's. Her afternoon shift after she'd finished at the workroom."

Culley removed his foot and grinned. Poor Mum Maguire deserved her bingo: two sackings and this layabout clogging up her kitchen when she got home.

The car was in good nick after its service, the brakes tightened and the paintwork clean for once. He switched on the radio and idled in the rush-hour traffic, finding himself in a line of cars in a snarl-up outside the Adelphi Grill.

Dimitri's caff was in full swing, the windows steamy and

the blurred outlines of tables jammed with customers all lit up by mauvish strip lighting. Perhaps he should bring Marianne over here one night? Marianne was a sport: the sort to enter into the spirit of a rollicking blow-out in Brixton.

He froze. No mistake. The girl running out of the caff and jumping into the Alfa parked at the kerb was none other than Raymond Turner's blonde! The Alfa eased into the traffic just as the lights changed to green.

Culley kept her in sight, trailing the white sportscar as it tacked across the river, eventually parking on a residents' slot in Chelsea. She walked the few yards back to a travel agent's on the point of shutting up shop. Culley found a meter and sat tight, keeping the girl in full view as she stood at the counter. She was certainly taking her time about it. Planning a spring break in the Caribbean with her boss?

Culley puzzled over this stroke of luck – the sheer coincidence of spotting Turner's bint at the caff a million to one chance. No, ten million to one. What was she doing in Brixton? A little recce for Raymond or was there a deeper significance? Had this skinny blonde been involved in the Gordon woman's disappearance right from the start?

He decided not to risk trailing her home but to take the other option: find out her name and where she was jetting off to.

When she had driven off Culley hurried into the agency just as the girl was making a second attempt at closing up. He flashed his ID through the glass and she reluctantly let him in, locking the door behind him. A man appeared from a back office and after a swift exchange disappeared with the files from her folder, eyeing the policeman with curiosity.

Culley got swiftly down to business.

"The lady who just left. The blonde. The police are interested in her movements. Was she planning a trip?"

The girl looked startled. "Kimberley Carter? She's a regular client. Her company has an account with us. We deal with all Mr Turner's travel arrangements."

Kimberley Carter? Culley felt himself break out in a sweat. Blimey, that was one of the names in Wiffin's visitors' book. She had been at the Zelini sale the night of the fire . . .

"Mr Turner's going abroad?" he said evenly.

"The booking was a private one. For Miss Carter. Cash." She laughed nervously. "Funnily enough a one-way ticket. Perhaps she's going on somewhere else later . . . First class, of course. Last flight out of Gatwick Friday night. She booked a double room for a long weekend," she said and then, just for the hell of it, added, "The Danieli".

The words hung in the air, envy staining the innocuous phrases.

"Venice."

"So romantic in the spring," she said, giving a tight little smile.

Sixteen

Culley spent the next morning at Companies' House trying to check out the ramifications of the Turner empire. After an hour he gave up and rang a contact on one of the financial papers, a drinking pal from his dealing room days.

They met at a wine bar in the City, Tony Snelling's curiosity whetted at the prospect of renewing links with a former dealer turned cop. Whatever next? Tony looked as scruffy as ever, the dark suit crumpled, his old rowing club tie liberally spattered. But the smooth manner was much in evidence and the hack image, Tom Culley suspected, a deliberate pose. Tom had seen the guy off duty when the ratty business suit was substituted for slick designer gear, threads no down-at-heel reporter would be able to afford.

They settled in a corner booth. It was too early for the lunch crowd and the place was practically deserted. After an initial skirmish, Tom gave Snelling a peek at his current investigation, recounting the story of the Zelini fire and the problem of its nameless victim.

"But what really intrigues me is why on earth a bloke like Raymond Turner involves himself with these piddling outfits? Literally dozens: a third-class hotel in Scotland, a couple of restaurants, even a hairdressers' salon in Birmingham for God's sake. You name it."

Tony sipped his claret, all ears. "Who's the solicitor?"

"Turner's lawyers? There are several handling the small businesses, mostly provincial firms. I gave up counting. Why would a big noise like Turner *bother* with all these nickel and dime operations? I ask you!"

"Funny you should be involved with Turner – I've been nosing around on and off for the past couple of years but it's a bloody rats' nest, Tom, impossible to unravel."

"It only got to us because of the fire. And if this woman hadn't died the whole case would have been wrapped up straight off."

"Arson?"

"No evidence of it. Last time I spoke to Turner he was saying he was going to refinance the Zelini operation, pump even more capital in. Worth it do you think?"

Tony Snelling shrugged. "I heard Zelini was crap, all washed up bar the shouting. The only way to relaunch a sinking ship like that would be to get in a new young designer to give it a burst of publicity – a sparkler with sex appeal."

Culley swigged the last of his wine and was preparing to leave it at that, to dump it on Tony Snelling, who would give him a buzz if he heard anything interesting. As he pushed back his chair, his contact raised a hand, looking Culley straight in the eye.

"There could be another scenario for all this," he said.

Culley glanced at his watch and poured a glass of mineral water, knowing all too well that Kline would be on the warpath if he didn't put in an appearance at the station before noon. Also he'd promised himself a look at the current Turner development, Turner House, to try and find out more about Kimberley Carter, before he dashed back to Streatham to interview the cleaner, Mary Maguire, this afternoon.

"You ever heard of off-the-shelf companies, Tom?"

"Sure. A means of avoiding delays in registration."

"Most are used for legitimate purposes but there has, in recent years, been a feeling that they've been used to hide the identity of the owner of the assets."

"Go on."

"Solicitors and accountants set up these companies by providing Memorandum and Articles of Association to Companies' House with the names of two directors plus the initial capital. The named directors may be partners in the law firm and the initial capital may be say £100. Once satisfied, Companies' House will issue a Certificate of Incorporation and the 'off-the-shelf' is then available to trade the same day. Off-the-shelfs are available in many countries although they're more often associated with tax havens. When required, the company is sold on by the solicitor to an 'investor' and the directors may be changed, the shares of the company most likely being held by a nominee company or even a whole string of them so the real owner is very difficult to trace."

"What's this got to do with Turner Developments?"

"Believe it or not, people walk into a solicitor's office saying they wish to buy a property for cash through an off-the-shelf company. There is no reason to doubt that it is a perfectly legal transaction but it does leave the door open to illegal transactions."

"You're talking money laundering, aren't you, Tony?"

Snelling nodded. "If you chat up your police department handling this sort of naughtiness they'll tell you I'm not spinning a yarn here. Apart from British thugs wanting to launder their drugs earnings, criminals from South America and the Italian mafia are all known to launder cash through Britain. And banks dare not think of the opportunities which

118

will open up with the prospect of the single currency. All over Europe criminal gangs are whooping it up. During the changeover money laundering will be child's play – awkward cash transformed into sparkling Euros at a stroke. Sometimes these gangsters invest in legitimate businesses such as clubs or shops and then the solicitors can say they are only dealing in whiter-than-white cash transactions. Spreading the load through small local solicitors and provincial firms is an ideal cover because the police concentrate on the big boys in London."

"Do you know Raymond Turner? Is he the type to dabble in this sort of stuff?"

"Raymond Turner didn't get where he is by pussyfooting around. A self-made man – he would have done even better in the States but even here it's still possible to build an empire starting with a single brick. Born grafter. Started out in Brighton and bought his first house before he was twenty. Hard man – don't kid yourself an ex-futures dealer like yourself can pick up enough info to unravel Turner's bundle of knitting. I've tried. Still, if you've got any tips I'll have another dabble if you like."

This apparently magnanimous offer didn't fool Culley but being short of support in his sniper fire on Superintendent Ackroyd's investigation of the Griffith murder, establishing a link with the dead woman and the Zelini operation via Raymond Turner was worth a gamble. He gave Tony his home number.

"One other thing, Tom. Did you find out if Turner's had any dealings with the art market? Owns a gallery, for instance?"

"No. Nothing like that. Why do you ask?"

"Just idle curiosity. I'm doing a feature on money laundering via fine art dealing and wondered . . ."

Culley rose, giving Tony Snelling a cheerful slap on the back by way of farewell, leaving him to finish the bottle and wait for the regular clientele to join him in the lunch session.

While Culley was trawling his old City haunts, Solomon had persuaded Anabel to take the day off to explore the islands. It was a beautiful day, the sky rinsed clear azure by a sharp breeze, the waters of the lagoon rippling with the backwash of motor boats and private launches. They caught a *vaporetto* to Murano and allowed themselves to be wafted into a factory to watch glassblowers at work, the magical twirling of the glowing staves to form molten balloons of glass a sight bordering on alchemy.

Solomon was in his element squiring a pretty girl about in the sunshine and sharing his formidable knowledge of the Veneto. He wore jeans with a leather jacket, his eyes like chips of lapis in the clear light.

"I lived in Padua for a couple of years, travelled about a good deal – learned to drive like an Italian maniac, swear, and eye up the girls, of course."

Anabel's city pallor was already freshening, her skin glowing, her hair knotted with a red ribbon, its ends streaming in the wind.

They bought the ingredients for a picnic before they left Murano: wine, some ciabatta, mozzarella, tomatoes and fresh fruit, adding some plastic knives from a market stall and buying two exquisite tumblers from the glassworks as a memento. Anabel couldn't remember being so happy. She glanced at Solomon from under lowered lids, watching him stow the fragile glasses in his knapsack before insisting, despite her howls of protest, that their next excursion was to San Michele, the cemetery island.

In wonder, Anabel admitted the place had it own weird fascination, dotted with gleaming Carrara marble, its curious photographs of the dead guarded by dozens of carved angels in varying stages of decay. The two wandered hand in hand, Anabel excitedly exclaiming at the extraordinary tributes, Solomon translating the heartfelt epitaphs of the newly dead. The place was haunted by legions of scrawny cats who appeared and disappeared like smoke between the tombs and lines of dark cypresses.

"Most Venetians are only here for a while, laid to rest in funny little niches for no more than a dozen years or so," he said. "After that the bones are dumped elsewhere. A necessity."

"No room?"

"Exactly. There are those who are rich enough to buy a plot in perpetuity, of course, but the Venetians are a stoical lot – used to practical solutions."

Under the spell of the place Anabel found herself confessing her inescapable bondage. Ronnie. Her love. Her life. She collapsed against the warm trunk of a tree, feeling the wretchedness overwhelm her. Solomon waited for the mood to pass, then lay down beside her on the grass, stroking her hair, saying nothing.

At last he pulled her to her feet and they wandered on, entwined, looking for a quiet corner to eat their picnic. After a glass of wine Anabel lost her fears of their silent companions in the mausoleums, who were hemming in their makeshift spot. It was late afternoon before they returned to Venice and Solomon insisted they would dine out in style.

"I'll call back at nine. Wear something slinky. There's someone I want you to meet." Anabel dawdled over her bath, pointedly ignoring the draped canvas pushed into a corner, knowing all too well that Solomon was going to try to persuade her to throw up the commission and give her talent a decent chance.

Later, they were enjoying an aperitif by Alys's window and laughing at the antics of the neighbour with the parrot. Exhausted by the bird's screeching she had flung its cage back on the balcony.

"*Finito! Finito!*" it screamed as the cover was tossed over its prison.

The phone rang.

Anabel reached across Solomon, resting her hand on his shoulder.

"Hello?"

Suddenly she sprang up, gripping the receiver. The conversation was brief, Anabel's response terse with anxiety.

"Who was that, darling?"

"A friend. Calling from London. Solomon, I've got to get back straight away. Ronnie's in intensive care."

"That serious?"

She nodded.

"I'll come with you," he said, holding her painfully close as if to prevent her bolting on the spot.

Seventeen

It was three in the afternoon before Culley tucked away his modest vehicle in the underground car park below Turner House. He had nipped home to change, to put on one of his old City suits, a flash number with a silky sheen, no outfit for a copper. Straightening his tie in the rear view mirror he gave a wry smile as if to salute the reappearance of a persona he had almost forgotten. At least he looked like a punter well able to afford a flat in Turner House.

He emerged from the lift directly on to the top floor, still absorbed in the smallprint of the brochure. The penthouse suite commanded a panorama of a bend in the river and the impressive skyline on the opposite bank. For a split second Culley almost wished himself back in the dealing room, pocketing his megabucks salary, being a genuine contender when it came to buying a pad like this.

The show flat promoter, Andy Bailey, was putting out his spiel to a couple from Hong Kong, their inscrutable response driving him to even greater feats of persuasion. Culley filled in the time ranging round the tasteful interiors, admiring the special selling features: the fresh flowers, the aroma of coffee brewing in the kitchen.

Once the penthouse emptied, Andy Bailey joined Culley in the dining room and, after shaking hands with this promising new prospect, the super salesman got into his stride. Culley made all the right noises, giving nothing away, hinting only at his undeniable familiarity with international finance markets. Andy enthusiastically filled him in on other Turner Development projects in the pipeline including loft-style warehouse conversions down river.

"What brought this development to your notice, may I ask?"

Culley grinned, admitting, man-to-man, that, "Actually I met this girl in the travel agents. Kimberley. We got talking and she said she worked here."

Andy stiffened, seeing a crack in the role he had sketched out for this apparently caked-up prospective buyer.

"You know her, of course," Culley persisted. "Between you and me, is she a runner?"

Andy's smile evaporated, his smooth manner ruffled by this unexpected twist.

"Well, in confidence, Mr Culley—"

"Oh, call me Tom."

"Well, as I was about to warn you, Tom, Kimberley's sort of spoken for."

This olde-worlde phrase made Culley burst into laughter and Andy Bailey relaxed, slipping into an easy locker-room exchange with a bloke just like himself, a man with plenty of dosh, the sort he could relate to. They moved into the kitchen where Andy poured two cups of coffee which Culley laced with a shot from his hip flask and, in the absence of any other viewers, the two settled down to a macho chinwag, the ribald laughter bouncing off the walls, lending the sterile apartment a welcome humanity.

As Culley unlocked his car and set out for Streatham, he had to admit he was very little the wiser about Turner

Development's modus operandi or the relevance of Kimberley Carter, either as an employee or the boss's little bit of fluff. Andy Bailey was not the fool he pretended to be and, in fact, had given very little away. Still, it *was* made clear that Kimberley was more than just the bimbo in the Turner set-up. Andy credited her with being entirely in the entrepreneur's confidence, even in business deals.

"Don't let her air-brained performance convince you, chum. Kimberley's on the inside track with the big man. A smart cookie."

"And you? Are you on the inside track, Andy?"

"Looking for tips, Tom? The lowdown on any insider dealing on the horizon? Don't think the City boys haven't got their eye on Turner."

"But you're not tempted?"

Andy's handsome features darkened.

"I'd be an idiot to go behind Turner's back. No pay-off from a would-be shark would be worth the danger."

"He's a hard man I hear," Culley said, topping up the coffee from his flask.

Andy shook his head. "Only to those who cross him. Me? I keep my nose clean and make sure I stay close to the action. I'm due for a place on the board any day now."

"He's promised you that, has he?"

Andy visibly expanded, eyes glittering as he assured Culley that his career with the Turner Development Corporation was gilt-edged.

It gave Culley plenty to think about as he tacked from the South Bank to Mary Maguire's. The Lout, as Culley dubbed him, was having his tea, absorbed in a replay of last night's match. Mary herself was a surprise. Far from the downtrodden char Tom had envisaged, the woman was dressed in a smart polo-neck and grey trousers, no trace of dark roots in her stiff peroxide coiffure and only pink fluffy flippers to underline that it was now after working hours. Without asking, she set a mug of tea on the table for him and after her appeal to Wayne to turn the volume down, they got down to business.

Mary Maguire was a good witness, needing little prompting and giving no indication of bitterness at losing her job at the Zelini workroom after the fire.

"Bad luck, Miss Maguire. Jobs not easy to come by these days."

"It's not so bad. Anyway, I wasn't all that struck with being at the beck and call of that cow, Aynesley-Foster."

"The office administrator."

"Mr Cayster was a good sort. Give me a month's wages in lieu when I got the push but I wasn't sorry to leave. It wasn't my week as it 'appens. Must have been something in me stars," she added with a chuckle.

"Wayne told me you lost your other job too."

"Same week! Don't know why I work for women – nothing but bitches. I should get out of this cleaning lark but the pay's good if you're willing to slog up West and I like to be flexible – while Wayne's not working, see."

"What happened? Not another fire, I hope?"

She giggled. "No such luck. I got this other cleaning job last summer like. Mrs Sagga. Often abroad she was. An Arab lady. Beautiful house and plenty of staff not like that skinflint Madame Zelini. I used to pop over there afternoons when I'd finished at the workroom. Just a couple of hours, a bit of ironing, general tidying up jobs, nothing much to it really. Mrs Sagga had gone back home for a visit and I thought the place was empty. Trouble was no-one told me that that sister-in-law of hers was staying overnight on her way to Paris. The Saggas have this guest suite, see. On the top floor. The family use it when they're passing through London. Well, on my way over to the Saggas' place I stopped off in the market for a nice bit of pork for my Wayne's tea. Thinking there was no-one there, I popped my shoppin' in the fridge at the Saggas' and was getting on with my work upstairs when there was this bloody racket in the kitchen. Screaming her head off she was, bawling out the poor little Filipina who does the rough and believe me that kid's no match for people like that. I went down to see what's what and, blow me, she'd thrown my loin of pork out the window and was beating the poor bloody maid about the head like she was a punchbag. Quick as a flash, I see what's causing the trouble and get between the two of them and tell this other Mrs Sagga it was all my fault. Give me notice straight off, no messing, no pay-off like Mr Cayster tipped up, and me, being quick tempered like, go storming out the house. Even forget me overall, left it when I put my coat on and haven't had the nerve to go back for it. Nice pinny an' all. A present from Mrs Sagga at Christmas – the real Mrs Sagga that is," she added with asperity. "No reference either, worse luck."

Seeing a glimmering of guilt winking away behind the outrage, Culley popped the stock question in the Zelini staff interrogation routine.

"Now, please think about this, Miss Maguire. Did you ever, at any time, distribute any printed invitations to the sale? Two are still unaccounted for. It sounds trivial, I know, but I must ask you just to square my records."

Mary Maguire flushed, the colour rising under her rouged cheeks, a roar from Wayne's TV soccer match exaggerating the silence as Culley waited for an answer.

"Well, to be honest, Sergeant, I did nick a couple of invites. Just to show my friend Doreen who's mad about clothes. I found two smudged ones in the bin at Zelini's and slipped them in my overall. Showing off really – Doreen didn't believe I worked there, see. Thought I was 'aving her on."

Culley breathed a sigh of relief, smiling broadly at the woman across the table, patting her hand in reassurance.

"No problem, Miss Maguire. Just let me have them, would you?"

"I can't."

"Oh? Why's that?"

"Like I said, I flounced off out of the Saggas when she threw my meat out and forgot to take me overall. The invites are still in the pocket."

Culley rose, gathering his papers, assuring her he would be back with a statement for her just as soon as he had reclaimed the printed invitations.

"I'll get your overall while I'm about it, if you like. The Saggas won't want it, will they?" he laughed. He jotted down the address and checked the time. The reclamation of the last two missing cards could wait until tomorrow. More urgently he needed to get more information about Raymond Turner's girlfriend – call in on Gordon's landlord and find out what Kimberley Carter was doing at his caff last night. It was all too coincidental – the mysterious links connecting Turner, the blonde, the artist woman and poor dead Abigail Griffith, not to mention the unfortunate shopper caught up in the Zelini fire.

When he arrived at the Adelphi Grill the place was gearing up for the evening rush, a bunch of hungry scaffolders hunched over their egg and chips, the place hazy with cigarette smoke. Culley pushed Dimitri into the back room and jumped straight in with both feet.

"What was that blonde doing here last night? Kimberley

Carter. Smart chick in the Alfa. Don't pretend you've got amnesia, Georghiou."

Dimitri's forehead glistened with sweat, his protestations rising in decibels, his wife, a big lady with muscles like a weightlifter, bursting in, demanding to know what was going on.

Culley pushed her out, flashing his warrant card, his temper rising.

"The woman who came to fetch the package for Annie? She never told me her name. A friend she said. The post for the flat upstairs come 'ere – the postman he likes a coffee when he comes by. You know?"

"On whose say-so did you pass over this package?"

"She phoned me herself. Said give it to her friend."

"Sure it was Anabel Gordon?"

"Course I'm sure! What do you think of us – Greek thick'eads?" But Culley's belligerent stance cut him short. "Well, the line was bad I admit. But it *was* Annie – my wife'll tell you – she spoke to her too. That's when she said she was in Venice."

Culley drew in a sharp breath, his mind racing.

"What was in this parcel?"

"How would I know?" he pleaded.

"Drugs?"

Dimitri stiffened, his tone sparking dangerously, the veins in his neck bulging. "There are *never* no drugs on my premises," he said with finality.

"And Anabel Gordon's not a user?"

"No way!"

"A supplier?"

"Never!"

"You're telling me, Georghiou, Gordon has no contacts at

all with the drugs scene? Pull the other one, mate – a party girl like that, shooting off to Italy at a moment's notice."

"Well," he admitted, "apart from a druggie in Kings Cross I heard she visits most weeks."

"Could she be supplying this person?"

"No! She ain't got no money for drugs. Even got her phone cut off and never up to date with the rent. Ask Renée if you don't believe me."

"Come off it, Georghiou. She earns big bucks on the art game, I hear. Why's the landlord last on her payout list? Did she settle her rent before she skipped? You sure she's not financing a habit? Or a boyfriend's habit?"

"Sure!"

"Does she often take off abroad like this?"

"It's work not 'olidays. She'll be back in a few weeks." Dimitri shook his head in irritation.

"And she told you all this when she phoned to say her friend would be calling in for the parcel. You said nothing to me about her zipping off to Venice when I spoke to you before."

"I only knew about it yesterday."

Culley looked sceptical. "Well, what is this address?"

Dimitri copied it into his order book from a calendar on the wall by the phone and tore off the page, handing it over with a scowl.

"Did the blonde give it to you? The address in Venice?"

"No, Annie, she give it to Renée. The girl didn't ask at first but after she'd been gone five minutes she come running back looking all panicky to check the address with me just to make sure she had it right she said. She wrote it on the empty envelope from the parcel. I wasn't happy about that."

"Why not? Did Anabel tell your wife not to tell anyone?"

"No. Anyway, the lady was meeting up with her for the

weekend, she told Renée. But why had she opened Annie's parcel? We don't want Annie to think *we* had been nosing into her private stuff. Annie told us on the phone her friend was just picking it up for her."

"Did she take the rest of Gordon's post?"

"I forget to give it her. I should have give her a message for Annie, to tell her about the lawyer ringing up askin' why Annie hasn't been in to sign the insurance claim."

"What insurance claim?"

Dimitri shrugged.

"And this blonde's a friend of hers, she said. Been here before? Not the sort of looker you'd forget, is she, Georghiou?"

"Can't say. Might 'ave."

"Well you'd better hand it over – the rest of the post."

"I can't do that!"

"I'll give you a receipt. You don't want to go down for obstructing the police in a murder investigation, do you?"

"Murder? What fuckin' murder?"

"Your lodger's other friend was beaten to death just before the girl scarpered abroad. I need to find out what her hurry was."

"I'll go ask Renée for her mail," he muttered, disappearing into the kitchen. Voices were raised. After a few minutes the muscle-bound wife burst in waving a bundle of letters.

"Dimitri he say Anabel in trouble. No way she into drugs! I *know* that girl, she like my own daughter." Her eyes bulged, the lodger's mail clasped to her chest like a trophy. Culley calmly penned a receipt and held out his hand for the letters and, ignoring her fury, aimed one last thrust.

"This girl Kimberley Carter who was here last night. Been here before, Mrs Georghiou?"

"Annie has her own front door. How we know who comes and goes?" she retorted.

"You could have told me your lodger had gone to Venice and saved us a lot of time."

"Didn't know till yesterday, did we? Only when she phoned. She ain't a kid you know, Sergeant. Don't have to tell us all her business."

"Fair enough."

Culley pocketed his pen and notebook and shoved the letters in his briefcase, grinning at the exasperated duo just to prove there were no hard feelings. Getting hold of Gordon's mail was a bonus. With luck the letters would prove the final link in this chain of events.

In fact, the letters were a let-down, the lawyer's directive proving nothing except the girl had been at the fire and was pursuing an insurance claim, nothing to further the investigation. The rest of the stuff was mainly bills, nothing from the girl's junky boyfriend in Kings Cross, nothing to indicate that Anabel Gordon was involved in drug running. Even so, the association between Kimberley Carter and the runaway was a facer. If he could only fold up the Zelini case and identify the dead woman from the fire he might, with luck, still be able to wangle his way on to Ackroyd's team – convince the silly old fart he had some valuable input in the Griffith case.

Eighteen

B y the time they had flown to London and got to the hospital Ronnie was dead.

The ward sister drew Anabel to a side room.

"Veronica never regained consciousness, I'm afraid. An overdose. There was nothing you could do."

"I came as soon as I could," she blurted out. "Ronnie's neighbour rang me in Venice. She found my number by my sister's phone."

The words came tumbling out as if to explain. But there was nothing to explain. It was all too clear. She had come too late.

"You're working abroad Mrs Tripp told us. I am so sorry, Miss Gordon. You are the only relative?"

Anabel straightened, swallowing hard. "Yes."

"Please come with me. We have laid out the body in a separate ward."

Anabel joined Solomon outside and in silence they trooped through a maze of corridors to a prefabricated building next to the hospital chapel. They waited in a dim ante-room, Anabel suspecting that the so-called separate ward was, in fact, the mortuary. Solomon gripped her shoulders as if fearing she would faint, the undeniable antiseptic smell of the place permeating the flimsy structure like a miasma.

After a few moments an orderly wheeled in a trolley draped in a sheet, Ronnie's beautiful face serene, her gaunt cheeks sculpted in death as if she were a carved angel. It reminded Anabel of the stone angels at San Michele. Perhaps San Michele had been some sort of warning. Ronnie looked at peace, at peace as Anabel could never remember her. The girl lying on the trolley was no longer anyone she knew. For a fleeting moment Anabel felt only release, the unknotting of a terrible constraint. Silent tears trickled down and, closing her eyes, she turned aside, hiding her face in Solomon's jacket.

He led her away, back to his flat, insisting she took one of his sleeping pills, and left her to dissolve the numbness in sleep. When she woke they found they were both ravenous and sent out for Chinese, the myriad choices going some way to assuage the shock of Ronnie's violent end. Perhaps it was inevitable. Perhaps Veronica Gordon had come to the end in her own mind. Anabel thrust these thoughts aside – it was all too soon.

Over the coffee, conversation was almost normal.

"What were you doing living in Padua?" she asked.

"Oh, that was years ago – I was not long out of college. I wanted to study Italian decorative painting. Trompe l'oeil, marbling and so on."

Anabel whooped with delight, hugging the big man like a prize teddy won at a rifle range.

"What brought that on?" he said, laughing.

"Don't you see? You've just admitted to being a fraudster. Just like me!"

"Trompe l'oeil's not the same and you know it."

"Come off it, darling. If the object is not to deceive, why do it?"

"It's a joke! It's a trick that fools nobody. Painting a wall to look like marble pillars or jazzing up a plain ceiling to seem as if it's a circular balcony peopled by curious onlookers and putti is merely a decorative device – no fucking fraud." He was clearly needled.

"But it is a deceit none the less. What I do is no worse."

"You're off your trolley, Anabel. What you do is so good it tricks a buyer into thinking he's got the real McCoy."

"No it doesn't. Some commissions are like the Cicely Alexander – for someone who's fallen in love with something clearly unattainable."

"Methinks the lady protests too much."

"Try to be serious, Solomon – it's important to me."

"Look. I deal exclusively in contemporary art. The buyer gets to meet the artist, the work is imbued with brushstrokes which are part of the painter's personality. When a punter signs a cheque and takes one of my pictures home, he buys a bit of the artist and, chances are, if he lives with the work long enough he will want another picture from the same studio – another chunk of the artist. What you do is merely a *reflection* of another man's work. You deliberately submerge your own talent to mirror another's style and whether it's an obvious copy like the Whistler or a deliberate fraud, the dishonesty is a criminal act against the artist. I'm not concerned with the people who are defrauded or the money to be made by crooked dealers – to me the sin is against the original artist, be he dead or alive."

Solomon's diatribe hit Anabel right between the eyes and she edged away, knowing his criticism to be fair. He drew her back, caressing the nape of her neck, murmuring assurances that she mustn't let people like Philip Barclayson ruin her talent. He tried to persuade her to cosy up but her agitation was palpable. She leaned back, closing her eyes, grasping fistfuls of her wild hair in a gesture of pure frustration.

"How on earth did you get into this game in the first place?"

"Money. Why else? I needed the money."

"For Ronnie?"

"Not at first but then later . . . You have to understand about Ronnie. She was always, well, 'my child'. I was twelve years old when our family bombshell arrived."

"Your ma's little mistake," he said with a grin. "Bit like my little Freddie."

"More than that. My Dad walked out – knew straight off the kid wasn't his. Her boyfriend moved in with us for a month or so – no longer. They rowed all the time and the baby was sickly, always crying."

"So Big Sister got lumbered."

Anabel demurred. "Actually it was more like having a real live doll and as Mum was always out nights working I—"

"A barmaid?"

"How did you guess?" she bitterly retorted. "Anyway, as she got older Ronnie was always getting the thick end of her tongue – I guess Mum blamed her for the mess we were in. Then, when Ronnie was fifteen or so, we got a real live 'live-in-Dad' and Mum thought we'd be a normal family again."

"Then what?"

"They didn't get on, of course they didn't. As a stepfather Alan was a bastard but Mum liked him. Ronnie started skiving off school, staying out nights – I'd left home by then so she had to stick up for herself. Then she got pregnant. That did it. Alan threw her out. She stayed with me for a bit but she was already snorting and, I suspect, on the game to pay for it. That's when I got an offer for a copy job."

"A dealer?"

"Yeah. Bloke up in Northampton wanted this Tudor portrait copied and I did it on the spot. The dealer took it away for 'final touches' and I got paid in cash."

"By the dealer?"

Anabel nodded.

"And he was?"

She shook her head. "Sorry, I forget. It was a one-off and after that I started advertising for more work. Couldn't believe the demand. Seriously, Solomon, there are people out there who'd pay anything to kid themselves they've got a genuine masterpiece up there on the wall."

"And you supply this rotten trade?"

"Why not? It paid for Ronnie to go into a rehab centre and after the baby was born I thought she'd change."

Solomon sighed, seeing the pain tearing her apart.

"But, wouldn't you guess, with Ronnie's bad luck things wouldn't pan out that simply? The baby died."

"How?"

"Cot death. Only eight months old and the sweetest little thing you ever saw. The social worker was sceptical – aren't they always? But Ronnie had tried, Solomon, she really had tried. After that it was downhill all the way. Back on the needle. Back on the streets. I never knew who was squatting in her flat, the place was a shit heap."

She wiped her eyes with a wodge of tissue, staring out at the leaden sky, utterly wrung out.

"But you kept on – supplying her with money, indirectly feeding her habit," he persisted.

Anabel leapt up, stung, her inertia instantly swept away. "Yes. I bloody well did. And don't think I didn't hate her for it often enough. But it was all my fault, leaving her like I did."

"What about her mother? She bears some blame in all this you know."

"Alan took her to Australia. I don't even know where they live now and I'm certainly not sending up any distress flares at this stage."

"What about the funeral?"

"What about it?"

"They might want to see you, to heal the breach. For all you know your ma might be suffering the agonies of the damned after leaving you to cope with your sister on your own."

Anabel's look bore all the cynicism of ten years steeped in misery. She reached out with both hands.

"Solomon, my darling. You are, in the nicest possible, way, an utter fool."

Nineteen

Tom Culley got on to Maguire's former employer, Mrs Sagga, first thing.

The house was a double-fronted residence on three floors with canopied steps leading up to the front door, paintwork gleaming and a tub each side of the entrance, colourful with spring bulbs. No expense had been spared and from an estate agent like Andy Bailey's viewpoint it was 'a prime property in mint condition'.

The door opened immediately, a bird-boned Filipina smiling shyly as she invited him into the tiled hall. He asked to see Mrs Sagga but the girl remained silent, merely smiling even more sweetly before disappearing downstairs. The house was very quiet and Culley wondered if the maid had understood a word he said. With luck she was fetching someone more vocal.

A housekeeper appeared from the basement area with the girl in tow, and Culley's hopes lifted. He introduced himself to the woman he assumed was the major-domo in the Sagga set-up and produced his ID. The response was immediate.

"Mrs Sagga asked you to come?"

"Er – no. I'm calling on a routine inquiry, a small matter I assure you."

The housekeeper looked sceptical and signalled to the girl to get back downstairs.

"Mrs Sagga only got back last night but she is expecting you. I'll take you up, shall I?"

Culley trailed upstairs behind her, confused by his reception. Kline knew he was calling here this morning but why would he warn the Saggas? He was shown into a drawing room overlooking the square, a luxuriously appointed salon furnished with ornate gilded chairs and too many mirrors. A bowl of exotic blooms displayed on a pedestal struck a dramatic note but the air was scentless, almost sterile in fact.

Mrs Sagga rose to greet him, a handsome woman, equally handsomely dressed in a ruby-coloured suit, her person generously arrayed with gold jewellery. She seemed anxious to ease her mind and after an apologetic examination of his warrant card, invited Culley to join her at the fireside. The room was oppressively hot and he felt a trickle of sweat run down his spine.

"You have come about my sister-in-law, I presume."

"No, madam, not at all. As I explained to your housekeeper I am here on a minor inquiry to confirm a statement from a former cleaner of yours, a Miss Maguire. There has been no formal complaint about your sister-in-law, I assure you."

Complaints about the ill-treatment of domestic staff working in foreign households had been much in the news lately. Did this lady think the Maguire female had concocted some story about brutality? Or reported the Saggas to an industrial tribunal? The little Filipina certainly hadn't the nous to make any legal moves.

The woman looked tired, her response strained, but she politely gestured him to continue.

"Miss Maguire, if you remember, was working here until

recently – light housework in the afternoons. She was summarily dismissed and left her overall in the kitchen. I would like to have it, if I may?"

Mrs Sagga's jaw dropped. "She sent a policeman to recover an apron?"

Culley tried to explain but Mrs Sagga impatiently rang a bell for the maid and eyed the sergeant with undisguised hostility. The girl appeared and went away again to fetch Mary Maguire's nylon pinny. As soon as she had gone Mrs Sagga recovered her poise and launched into an entirely unrelated matter, clearly the problem she had assumed had brought the police here in the first place.

"You see, Sergeant, my husband has been worried about our sister-in-law, Zain. It was Zain who dismissed the cleaning woman you mentioned. She has an unfortunate manner, unused to European ways with staff and I'm afraid her temper got the better of her. A religious scruple you understand?"

Culley nodded, clearly at sea.

"My housekeeper explained all this to me last evening but my husband had already been concerned about Zain not answering our calls to the Paris apartment. I assumed he had asked the police for help."

"Please forgive me, madam, but I am a bit mixed up here. Perhaps you could explain in more detail?"

She clasped her hands in an effort to compose herself and edged her chair a little nearer, lowering her voice to a tone of near-conspiracy.

"Zain came here for a few days while we were away – I'm not sure of the exact dates but Mrs Bellamy can tell you. Zain was flying on to Paris to do a little shopping and was expected to stay at a small apartment we lease for the family. I have to explain that my sister-in-law is what we would regard as a very modern young lady, someone used to her own way and impatient of the restraints which women of my generation grew up with. Zain is an enthusiastic shopper, I am afraid, and wastes much time and money attending fashion shows in Paris and New York. When your policewoman telephoned her over a week ago to check whether Mrs Sagga was at home, my housekeeper assured her that I had gone abroad but that she had spoken to me only that morning. A misunderstanding, of course, perfectly obvious in retrospect but naturally Mrs Bellamy thinks of me as Mrs Sagga and gave the matter no thought until my husband questioned her last night. It was only when we realised that Zain was not in Paris, and in fact had never arrived there, that we began to worry and it occurred to me when you were announced that you were following up some previous inquiries?"

"You have no staff at the Paris flat?"

"None. The concierge has an informal arrangement but the place is extremely small, Sergeant, and we hardly use it ourselves."

Culley's head swam. At that moment the maid returned with Mary Maguire's yellow overall and handed it to her employer. Mrs Sagga dropped it on the coffee table and resumed speaking, anxiety snagging her perfect English in her rush to continue. Culley raised a hand and, excusing himself, reached for the overall neatly folded on the low table. He shook it out and, feeling the empty pockets, said,

"Has this been laundered?"

She sighed and rang the bell again and this time the housekeeper appeared.

"Mrs Bellamy. Has this item been washed?"

"No, madam."

"You're sure?" Culley barked.

She nodded. "I put it in my own cupboard until Mary came for it. It was her favourite," she added.

"And you removed nothing from the pockets?"

She drew herself up. "Of course not."

Culley dipped into his case and produced a Zelini sale invitation.

"Nothing like this?"

The housekeeper faltered and, Culley would bet on it, hesitation had set in. She took the card and examined it closely, addressing her employer directly, ignoring Culley.

"Well, now that I see it, I did find two of these on the floor in the kitchen, madam. I found out later that Mary got the sack if you understand me – took off in a huff by all accounts. She threw off her overall and when I found these blank invitations half under the fridge I assumed they belonged on the hall table with the post."

"You had no idea where they came from?"

"The maid is new and rather nervous. I thought she had dropped the cards when she was sorting the post. I gave no heed to it, madam." The woman continued resolutely to address all her remarks to Mrs Sagga, a note of appeal sharpening her words to a knife-edge as the possible connotations of this unconsidered action focussed.

Mrs Sagga smiled. "One more thing, Mrs Bellamy," she said. "Can you tell the sergeant when Zain arrived and when she left? And when exactly you received the telephone call from the police?"

The housekeeper trotted out all the dates as if she had total recall, the confident manner now raw with anxiety.

"And when my constable telephoned to ask for Mrs Sagga you assumed she referred to your employer of course?"

"Naturally! I told her Madame was away but I had spoken

to her that morning and would give her a message next time she called. The policewoman said that wouldn't be necessary."

Culley turned back to the lady of the house, raising an eyebrow.

"That will be all, thank you Mrs Bellamy," she said. The woman left.

Culley spoke again. "Have you any recent photographs of your sister-in-law, Mrs Sagga?"

She quickly rose, taking a small studio portrait from a silver frame, handing it to him with trembling fingers. He glanced at the picture: a dark-eyed beauty dressed in a silver lamé evening gown, her hair threaded with a gold filet.

His pulse racing he extracted some photographs from his document case and spread them across the table.

"This jewelled locket, Mrs Sagga. Did your sister-in-law own anything like this?"

"I believe so. It was a gift. I only saw it once."

"And the name of the donor?"

"Zain could not say. She was something of a tease, Sergeant. You see, my brother-in-law is older and very indulgent of his new young wife. She told him it was an anonymous Valentine's Day present. All nonsense, of course. We don't celebrate such silly western occasions and obviously Zain had bought it for herself. She lavished a great deal too much on herself in our opinion: clothes, jewels, constant visits to Paris and Rome. Perhaps my brother-in-law tried to put his foot down? Is that the right term? We were used to Zain's little tricks and certainly did not believe this ridiculous story about some nameless admirer sending such a very expensive gift. Quite unacceptable to our culture and obviously a childish act of defiance on Zain's part."

Mrs Sagga was now clearly disturbed, glancing at the photo-graphs on the coffee table, her mind permutating the possible reasons, all unpleasant, which had brought this policeman to her door.

"Is Mr Sagga in London at present, may I ask?"

"Yes, of course. He has an import/export business here." She searched her handbag and passed him an engraved business card. "His office number, Sergeant. Do I assume that my sister-in-law's disappearance is now under investigation? We had no idea she was missing, you see. Not until last night. We thought she was in Paris and her husband assumed she was safe here in London. Zain is a law unto herself. Please let me know as soon as you find her. I hardly slept last night, worrying about the silly girl. But she has friends the family did not approve of. I'm sure she has just slipped off with her friends on a little holiday, knowing we might be cross with her if we found out."

Culley wrote a receipt for the overall and made his way out. No point in dragging Mrs Sagga over to the mortuary – the charred remains would have to be viewed by the brother-in-law, poor devil.

There was still the question of Wiffin's visitors' book. Filling in a blank card for herself was easy enough but had the Sagga name featured on the official list? This Zain woman could have phoned Zelini's to say she would come . . . Had anyone checked the list that thoroughly or had they all, like himself, been solely concerned with the women who had not, like Mrs Sagga, been accounted for as being alive and well? With hindsight, Culley had to admit his perusal of the names crossed off in the post-blaze ring-round had been careless. If it was true that two blank invitation cards had fallen out of Maguire's overall pocket when she'd stormed out and if, as

Mrs Bellamy had admitted, the cards had been left out on the assumption that they belonged to their house guest, then from what Mrs Sagga had to say about her fashion-freak relative, the prospect of filling in a blank evening with a trip to a private designer sale would have looked very appealing.

Clearly the younger Mrs Sagga came and went at will and was under no polite duress to inform the housekeeper she was staying out all night or even had gone for good. The lifestyles of these rich globetrotters was hard to imagine. On the one hand the glamorous young wife was spoilt rotten but on the other she was presumably frantically rigorous in her religious dietary laws and, once home, reverted to respectable Arab wife.

Culley started up the car, eager to get back to the station and brief Kline on this astonishing breakthrough.

In a matter of hours the poor Saggas had identified the body and, cock-a-hoop with the closure of the case, Kline readily agreed to allow his detective sergeant the week's holiday due to him. In fact Culley suspected Kline was more than anxious to see him off the premises, leaving the DCI to finalise the statements and presumably shape the report to shine a spotlight on the Kline leadership of a successful investigation.

Culley wasted no time booking his flight to Venice.

Twenty

When Anabel arrived at her flat on Saturday morning the door stood an inch ajar. The lock had been jemmied. She flew into the cafe to fetch Renée who trundled upstairs ahead of her, primed for action. The place had been ransacked.

"Did the police leave it like this?"

"I would have knocked their stupid 'eads together! No, Annie, this must have happened last night. The kids round here!"

They toured the rooms closing drawers, righting tables, trying to assess the damage.

"Looks worse than it is. Nothing seems to be missing – not that there was much here in the first place, I'd taken most of my stuff with me."

Renée insisted on helping her clear up; then went down to the caff to collar one of the builders who was just polishing off a fry-up. She came back with two mugs of coffee and a hefty slice of apple pie and insisted Anabel took the weight off her feet "while Charlie fixes up your door. You can get a new lock if you like but Dimitri thinks it'll be OK. You stayin'?"

"No. I only came back for my sketchbook. I'll stay over at Solomon's till after the funeral then I've got to fly back. To finish my commission."

Renée winked. "This Solomon. Your new boyfriend?"

"Sort of." She flushed. "For now anyhow. He's been very kind but he likes to take charge. Know what I mean? Wants me to move in with him, take a year off and try out some of my own ideas. Solomon owns a gallery. Could be my big break," she added with a comic grimace.

"Then you take it, Annie. As I'm always tellin' my Dimitri, it's not the jumps you takes that leaves the bruises but the jumps you too scared to try."

"Trouble is, Renée, I've sort of got used to looking after myself. As well as trying to look after my sister all these years. Not that I made much of a job of either as it turns out." She choked back the tears, unwilling to break down in front of Renée.

"Why you not tell me about your Ronnie? I thought it was some junky boy you visit, not family."

Anabel made a stab at the apple pie. "I suppose I was ashamed. Ronnie was always in trouble and it all seemed to be my fault – not being there for her, getting fed up with the bloody awful mess she was in. It turned her into a different person, Renée, not nice at all a lot of the time." She blew her nose.

Renée patted her hand. "Not her fault, poor child. But this new man of yours? He knew about your sister?"

"Mmm. Actually, he's paying for the funeral. God knows how I would have managed otherwise. Thanks for fixing the door, Renée, I'll get back to you but I've got to run – I've got a special appointment to see that solicitor at eleven about my insurance claim. He's coming in specially. If I get compensation I can pay Solomon back." She told Renée about the fire, showed her the almost healed scar on her thigh, and tried to make her leap in the dark from Zelini's first-floor window sound amusing. Renée didn't laugh. And Anabel didn't mention her acquisition of the crocodile handbag.

"This friend of yours who come for the package. She say she go to Venice to take it to you. But you leave before she got there, eh?"

Anabel nodded, unperturbed. "Yeah. Doesn't matter. It wasn't anything important."

"She look mighty worried girl when she come back for your address."

"My address in Venice?"

"Sure. Why not? You not want your friend comin' to your door?" Renée pursed her lips, her massive forearms folded on the table. "That policeman thought you was peddlin' drugs."

Anabel laughed. "Culley? He's an imaginative sod. Last thing I'd get involved in with Ronnie on my back." She polished off the pastry with a flourish and put on her coat.

"I've got to rush now, Renée, but you can reach me at Solomon's till after the funeral on Wednesday." She scribbled a telephone number on the corner of a magazine and Renée clasped her lodger in a breath-defying hug.

"You take care now. Dimitri will make sure them vandals keep away from your doorstep from now on. He got friends in the market – they got their finger on all the naughty boys round here."

She thumped off down the stairs and, after taking a last look round, Anabel followed her out, amazed to see her front door nailed up good as new again.

Culley had been to Venice before – several times in fact. That last time with Gerry, a miserable weekend break in November, the rain ruining Gerry's new stilettos. But it hadn't spoilt Venice for him. The raddled old Queen of the Lagoon was still beguiling, the flaking ochre walls flanking the Grand Canal more theatrical than any backdrop.

He booked into a little Austrian hotel he knew, a stone's throw from St Mark's, and, after leaving his luggage, changed into chinos and a denim jacket and sauntered over to the Rialto for a pizza. The tables were set out at the edge of the water, sheltered from a spring breeze by the bridge itself and giving a close-up of the passing launches and occasional gondola. He sipped his wine, relaxing in the sunshine, turning over in his mind the best way to approach Kimberley Carter in her four-star hideout.

He had no reason to consider her in hiding but the signals were there all right. And who was sharing this private excursion of hers if not Raymond Turner? Andy Bailey had been in no doubt that crossing the big man was dangerous and, reflecting on his brief interview in the boss's office, Culley had no reason to doubt it.

The hour after lunch was quiet apart from the tourists, bleeding every expensive minute from their holiday. Culley approached the Danieli with no little hesitation, still undecided how to play it. In fact, he need not have worried. The man on reception was adamant.

"Miss Carter checked out this morning, sir. So sorry." Culley felt as if the rug had been pulled out from under his feet.

"She's left Venice?" he barked.

"This morning, sir."

"Alone?"

"I could not say." The man was a professional to his fingertips, the eyes blank as pebbles, gigolos looking for lonely girls being two a penny in this town. It was hopeless. Culley knew when he was beat but, refusing to give the man on the desk the satisfaction of seeing his backside wend its way back on to the street, strolled into the bar and ordered a bellini.

The place was practically deserted and the barman, a refugee from the Fulham Road, was happy to relax with an English barfly. After a second cocktail and an espresso just to clear his head, Culley admitted defeat and wandered out into the sunshine again. Having lost his quarry in the first hour he was far from certain how he intended to spend this busman's holiday after all. It had never occurred to him that Kim Carter would give him the slip. His only other pointer was the Gordon woman's address and after consulting his guide book, Culley set off to find it. Perhaps the two girls had shacked up together? Two birds with one stone. He couldn't believe Kimberley had really gone back to England so soon. Anyway with a whole week paid for in advance he had nowhere else to go. Why not relax and enjoy?

Perked up by this happy thought and after several wrong turnings he finally located Anabel Gordon's current perch. No-one answered the door which didn't surprise him. From his scratching around in London he had formed a rough idea of the Gordon woman's means of making a living and this dark and narrow house jammed in a dark and narrow alley hardly looked the ideal situation for an artist's studio. But what did he know? Maybe she was a plein-air painter in which case where else would a charming vista present itself at every corner but in Venice?

"Bloody hell," he muttered. "She could be anywhere. And so could Turner's blonde."

After presenting herself at the lawyer's office and confirming the details of her losses and injury, Anabel reluctantly allowed herself to be quizzed about Abigail Griffith's death. The suite of offices was unattended, the empty rooms stuffy with the undeniable whiff of lost causes. The man was wearing a club blazer and flannels, just to impress on her his generosity in fitting her in at the weekend she supposed. The informality seemed to demand some leeway on her part, a bubble of moisture quivering at the corner of his mouth as he posed a series of embarrassing questions.

"Really, Mr Selkirk, I know less than anyone. I was in Italy when it happened. I only know what I read in the papers."

"But attacked in that brutal manner, half naked, tied to the lavatory? In *Hampstead*! Was your friend in the habit of letting strangers into her home? Orgies? Homosexual relationships are often, I hear, promiscuous, strangers having a special appeal, would you not agree?"

The man had an air of avidity about him, his eyes glittering. With repulsion Anabel found herself mesmerised by his ears which were large and extraordinarily hairy.

"Er, well – I wouldn't know. To be honest, Mr Selkirk, I never went there. We were more business colleagues, Gee-Gee and I."

This clearly disappointed him, having translated the dead woman's personal directive to deal with the Gordon compensation claim 'pronto' as a clear indication that a more interesting relationship between the two women was in progress. But Barry Selkirk was not a man to give up that easily – the delicious young lady edging away her chair was a rare bird in these chambers.

"You realise, of course, that there has been scandal in the press? One of the tabloids hinted at blackmail being a possible motive in such killings. VIPs caught on video – that sort of thing."

"Blackmail? Gee-Gee wouldn't even twist anyone's arm let

alone use blackmail!" Anabel leapt up, appalled by the web of intrigue which seemed to have enveloped a simple mugging. Was there more to it? Something she had missed while she had been obsessed by her own troubles? She determined to buy every Sunday paper on the rack this weekend. Whatever was this horrible man hinting at?

When she got back, her mind still whirring, she regaled Solomon with the story. He roared with laughter, stopping only to make Anabel tell it again. When they eventually got back on track he had another bit of gossip which shocked her even more.

"I really would advise you to chuck in this Barclayson commission, darling."

"Oh no, not again! Do you never give up? I agreed to do the Annie Haden portrait, Solomon, I've almost finished it and when it's done I promise you I'll take the cash and run. Dear God, I certainly need the money."

"Listen. I was chatting to a good friend of mine this morning. A TV bloke in Toronto. He gave me a hot tip. That researcher you said you met at the villa. His name came up."

"Matt Randall?"

"That's it! He's on a retainer. A deep throat investigation of art fraud. Very hush hush. And you say Philip Barclayson let this guy loose in his library while the rest of you lit out for Venice?"

"Alys stayed on."

"Maybe Alys knows. Maybe it was Alys who wangled him into Barclayson's confidence in the first place."

"Alys? Don't talk utter rubbish, Solomon. Alys has been with Philip for *years*. She wouldn't be party to a dirty trick like that."

"Big bucks, big talk."

"You sure you got the right man? I met this person. He's *nice*, Solomon. A real sweetie. No sort of media sewer rat."

Solomon looked thoughtful. "Well, you'd be a damned fool to get involved. Even if Philip comes up smelling of roses."

"Don't you tell me what to do! I've booked my flight straight after the funeral, Wednesday afternoon. Please don't let's discuss this any more, OK?"

Solomon shrugged and went down to his office in the basement. It was his weekend with his son, Freddie, coming up. Maybe it was just as well if Anabel was cooling off in Venice for another couple of weeks.

Culley found himself a bistro at the corner of Anabel's *calle*, tables and umbrellas set out in front, a discreet distance from the house where Kimberley Carter was sure to be.

The afternoon faded, pale stars glimmering in the dusk. No lights appeared in the empty building. After an hour he took a circuitous stroll, keeping an uninterrupted vigil on the shabby front door, returning to his table after a decent interval. He contented himself with the thought that if he was on duty there could be worse locations.

His patience paid off. When the cafe buzzed with diners and the narrow street rang with footsteps, a white blonde head bobbed into focus, dipping in and out of the crowd like a bubble on the surface of a lake. He swiftly closed in behind her and as she raised her finger to ring the bell, Culley closed his hand over her mouth and urgently whispered in her ear, "Please don't fight, Kimberley. It's Tom Culley – the policeman. I came to Turner's office, remember? If you agree, I'll let go and we can go somewhere for a quiet talk."

She vigorously nodded her head and, very carefully, still gripping her waist from behind, he removed his hand from her mouth. She turned to face him, her eyes filled with tears, and to his utter amazement, fell into his arms, grasping the lapels of his jacket for dear life, snivelling like a lost child.

People passing smiled, guessing at a lovers' tiff. Where but in Venice, after all? Famous for assassins and for lovers.

Twenty-One

K imberley Carter stumbled along beside Culley, holding on like a drowning woman. They went back to his hotel and he ordered steak sandwiches and coffee from room service. It had been a long watch since the pizza and, gazing at the wraith crouched on the sofa, he decided a slab of red meat wouldn't do her any harm either. He poured a shot of brandy for her from the mini-bar, which she downed like medicine, her eyes closing as if to shut out the light.

She wore a yellow dress, which on one of her good days probably suited her. And no make-up. In the unforgiving overhead light her pallor became sallow, her high forehead and angled cheekbones taking on the quality of ivory, only the heavily fringed eyelids softening the mask. But Culley had to admit that even in her current state of weariness the girl was a stunner.

He drew the curtains, muting the sounds of laughter from the street below, waiting for her to thaw out in her own time. The waiter who brought the sandwiches and coffee fumbled over the business of laying the side table, his curiosity overtaking professional dexterity as he covertly eyed the blonde reclining in the shadows apparently drunk or drugged, her silence unmanning his Italian brio. Culley asked him to top up the order with a bottle of scotch.

It took a lot of persuasion to get Kimberley to try the sandwiches, and the coffee remained untouched at her elbow. He drew up a chair to the table and played host as best he could, being well acquainted, post-Gerry, with girly moods. He turned on the radio, bathing the room with the soft strains of wallpaper music, and after the waiter had returned with the whisky he set about gaining her confidence.

He started off in a gentle vein, rabbiting on about Venice, asking her advice about restaurants. Kim focussed bush-baby eyes on him with growing attention, sipping her whisky, saying little. He offered her a cigarette and when they had both settled back, she put her first question.

"Are you tailing me?"

"Me?" Culley looked astonished as well he might, lying in ambush being more accurate. He described his casework on the Zelini blaze, the breakthrough in identifying the corpse catching her interest. She was coming alive at last.

"I was there you know."

"Yes, I know. You were lucky to get out."

"I've never been in a fire before. It's the most terrifying experience ever. That poor girl – burnt to death." She shuddered, stubbing out her cigarette with shaking fingers.

"Actually, she was dead before the flames reached her. She was killed by the fumes."

Kimberley looked relieved and resumed her robotic sips of whisky.

"What was wrong with the Danieli?" he prompted.

Her eyes widened. "You followed me there?"

"Not exactly. Were you expecting someone to join you?"

"He must have got delayed. I tried telephoning but his mobile's shut down."

"I thought you were with Raymond Turner." It was worth

157

a try, the girl seeming to be warming to him. Probably the whisky.

She sighed. "I was. I suppose I still am. But I fell in love with someone else. It's difficult."

"Yes, I can imagine. How long have you been with Turner?"

"Oh, ages. He picked me up at the place where I used to work. I was a manicurist at a barber's in St James's."

"But I heard you're more of a business partner in the development office these days."

"Well, yes. Raymond's very clever at picking people. Even me. I surprised myself, to be honest – always used to be bottom of the class at school."

Culley smiled. "I can't believe that."

"Yes, really." She uncurled her legs, leaning forward, a willing victim. "I'm slightly dyslexic, you see. Get words muddled up sometimes, get things just a bit off key. My memory's brilliant but between my brain and my mouth I get tripped up. That was how the trouble started with Anabel. I kept forgetting her name, mixing it up – Abby? Annie?"

His pulse quickened. "Anabel Gordon?"

"You know, the girl who's moved into that house where you picked me up tonight. The one with all that black curly hair."

Culley nodded. "I wanted to meet her myself. No luck so far."

Kimberley rattled on, getting into her stride at last, a sympathetic ear all she needed. "She's not in Venice you know. I've been ringing her every hour. I tried knocking her up tonight, thinking she was just lying low, but she's hiding out somewhere. I'll find her. I *must*. She works for an art historian, an old codger called Philip Barclayson. I made some enquiries about her while I was in London. He's got a place in Tuscany, a villa – I bet that's where she's gone. Would you come with me? We can hire a car at the airport. I'm so frightened, Tom."

"Was that why you left the Danieli? Because you were scared? Scared of Turner?"

"Why would I be scared of Raymond?" she bleated but tears welled up, caught in the fabulous lashes. Culley wondered if they were stuck on but quickly discarded this idle thought. Within the space of less than an hour he realised he was sunk: this girl was an angel from heaven, too beautiful for artifice. He dragged his attention back, assuring her he would drive her to the villa, help her find the elusive Gordon female.

"Tell me one thing. Why do you need to track her down?"

"She stole something which belongs to me."

"At the fire?"

Kimberley nodded, irritably brushing back a strand of hair. "My handbag."

Culley jolted, spilling whisky on his chinos. "Was it worth pursuing her across Europe for a handbag?"

She shrugged. "She said she'd parcelled it up for me but when I collected the package from her digs half of it was missing."

"You mean half the contents?"

"She posted the money and passports to that cafe in Brixton but nothing else. It means life or death to me."

"What does?" He topped up her glass, more confused than ever.

"It all started going wrong because of my dyslexia. Raymond trusts me with his personal files you see. He hates putting stuff on computer – terrified of hackers. So he keeps a record of his special transactions in an organiser – you know what I mean?"

159

"A sort of address book, the Sloany thing, right?"

"Yeah. Well, this organiser stays in a safe deposit box and I'm the only one allowed to fetch and carry the thing. My boyfriend got interested and being a stupid fool I said I'd get it for him. Raymond gave it to me to put back in the safe deposit and I said I would go there before I went on to the designer sale."

"You live with Raymond Turner?"

She nodded miserably. "He never lets me off the leash and being Raymond he's got these heavies who watch me all the time."

"I thought you said he trusted you?"

"He does. But recently I get the impression he suspects something."

"Your new man?"

She lowered her voice, her mouth quivering as she described the Turner set-up, her role doubling as office bunny and live-in lover.

"Raymond's *old* – know what I mean? I was dazzled at first but this new guy, well, you can guess the rest. Sexy."

"Someone you met in London?"

"Where else would I meet anyone?" she moaned, her anxiety ratcheting up several notches just thinking about cheating on Turner. "We decided it was getting seriously hairy – believe me, Raymond's not the forgiving type. My bloke promised to meet me round the corner from Zelini's about nine and we'd skip the country. Make a break and start up on our own in America."

"Why go to Zelini's at all?"

"I told you! I was being watched. One of Raymond's muscle men follows me in a van. I may be dyslexic but I'm not blind! I told Raymond I was going to the safety deposit place first, and I did but I kept the organiser back and went straight on to Zelini's like I said I would. I thought I'd be able to slip out the back which would give us a headstart. Raymond wasn't expecting me home till late. I told him I was meeting a girlfriend at the sale and we'd probably have supper together afterwards."

"Sounds reasonable."

"Everything would have been just fine except for that bloody fire." She started to shake, the ice rattling in her glass like chattering teeth. "I barely got out of there with my life, Tom. Really! And in the street everything was chaos: fire engines, crowds, the police, people screaming."

"So you lost your chance to escape."

She started to cry, big childish tears flopping down her cheeks. "Can I stay here with you, Tom? Just for tonight," she pleaded. He estimated his time was running out, the whisky aggravating some unspecified terror and set to douse his informant any moment now.

"Sure. But I'll need your passport. I know the proprietor, they'll be no problem." He rang down to reception explaining his dilemma, the night clerk succeeding in being both schmaltzy and efficient. They would send up the paperwork, no need for the young lady to check in downstairs at this hour.

He made instant coffee from the machine, doubling the strength, willing the fading beauty on the sofa to rouse herself. The fabulous eyelashes lifted and she resumed her narrative with renewed urgency, grasping Culley's wrist as if fearing he would jump ship.

"I got sort of whisked away from the fire, shoved in the van and sent back to Raymond's house like some sort of parcel."

"But you weren't hurt."

"No. Just jibbering with fright. First the fright of psyching myself up to leave Raymond and then having to go back to him knowing I'd lost all his files."

"It was the only record?"

"So I thought. He said it was too dangerous to keep copies and much too important to put on any computer disk."

"He must have trusted you implicitly."

She blew her nose, her eyes now rimmed with exhaustion.

"I told Raymond how I'd lost everything in the fire. My coat, my shoes, my handbag. He was so nice to me, Tom, so pleased to have me home safe, I had to stop myself running out there and then. Then I broke down and confessed I'd had the organiser in the bag that had gone up in smoke at Zelini's, said I'd forgotten to go to the safe deposit first as I promised. I could have bitten my tongue out as soon as I'd said it but it was too late – I'd remembered the bloke in the van who'd been tailing me. If he reported back to Raymond that I *had* gone to the safety deposit before going on to Zelini's, Raymond would know I was lying. I nearly passed out just thinking about it."

"But at first you truly believed the organiser had gone up in flames?"

"The police sifted the debris – nothing. Raymond accepted my story then admitted he had a duplicate after all, the pig. 'Not to worry my pretty little head.' That made me really mad. I got back to my boyfriend to explain why I'd moved back in with Raymond but he was worried about the thicko in the van reporting on my movements. We decided there was no time to lose – I'd have to leave first chance I got."

"What changed your mind?"

"That girl phoned me. The artist, Abby – Annie, whatever. She'd salvaged my bag and wanted to see me, put the bite on I guessed because of the passports and stuff. At first I thought,

Good. It's worth it. I'll get the organiser back and we'll revert to plan A."

"Whose passports? Yours and your boyfriend's?"

She shook her head. "Then Raymond set the dogs on me after the stupid girl sent a fax to Head Office and gave the game away. Raymond knew the organiser was back in circulation and that's when I made that tragic mistake. I got mixed up with her name – an honest to God slip of the tongue, Tom, I swear to you. I'm always doing it, Raymond used to think it was funny. When Raymond questioned me I called her 'Abby' – not Annie. I said I knew nothing else and I thought I could get the organiser back before Raymond got on to it. But Raymond got hold of the Zelini invitation list from the office and worked out who she was – this woman who was holding on to his property, trying to blackmail me. He came up with Abigail Griffith – it checked out in Wiffin's visitors' book and Raymond swore to sort her out."

"He *killed* Griffith?"

"Not personally. Sent two of his rottweilers to shake her down, I suppose. He denied it to me, of course, but he never expected that poor woman to hold out on him and it all went too far. What none of them knew except me was that Abigail Griffith wasn't even *there*. It was Annie Gordon at Zelini's sale – Griffith honestly didn't know *anything* or why they were torturning her. But they just kept turning up the heat, screwing her to the toilet and beating her brains out. Do you wonder I'm petrified?"

"Actually she died from a stab wound," Culley couldn't resist putting in, the perfectionist in him getting the upper hand. "Did you never tell anyone you'd got the name wrong? Someone with the same initials as it happened. You could have prevented Raymond from sending his thugs to her flat."

"I was scared witless – and anyway I had no idea they would do that. I didn't even tell my boyfriend it wasn't 'Abby'. He'd chickened out on me the night of the fire and I wasn't sure who to trust at first. When the Gordon girl called in at the show flat and left that bloody note everyone assumed she was just the 'gofer' for Abigail Griffith. I thought my slip of the tongue would give me time to contact the girl and get my stuff. It was only when that poor woman was found dead in her flat I panicked and told my boyfriend the truth."

"But not Raymond?"

"No. Later, when the dust had settled, my boyfriend and I decided to meet up here in Venice and pay off Annie and get the organiser back ourselves. But I guess he lost his nerve, left me here to stew on my own. Do you think Raymond found out who I'd been seeing – put the fear of God into the poor sap?"

Culley was about to dig further but at that moment the desk clerk knocked at the door, a leather folder in his hand, a goofy smile taking in the scene as he laid open the booking form before his befuddled prospective guest. Kimberley was clearly over the limit, a sweep of the hand bringing Culley to heel with her evening bag while she busied herself filling in the hotel register. He opened the bag which was barely large enough for her cigarettes and gold lighter.

There was only one passport inside and as he passed it over, Culley's eyes bulged. He was sharing a room with someone called Martha Ferrero? A Swiss? She signed in, smiling up at the clerk like a mermaid surfacing heavy seas. Culley meekly proferred his credit card to finalise this new arrangement and the man backed out to a smoochy radio rendering of the Skaters' Waltz.

Twenty-Two

He switched off the radio. After the desk clerk had gone Kimberley excused herself and tottered into the bathroom. Culley lit another cigarette, anxiously listening to the gushing of the shower, wondering if he could, if pressed, lie about the Swiss passport, pretend he knew nothing about it, he'd just picked up this blonde in the street on a one-night stand. He brightened with the fleeting thought that maybe her name really was Ferrero but sense prevailed as he gloomily stared at the carpet, juggling his options.

She emerged from the shower glowing, enveloped in the hotel's white towelling bathrobe, her hair bundled up in a towel, her terror presumably washed down the plughole judging by the relaxed new image.

Culley rose, feeling a bit of a berk, glad that at least the twin beds presented no embarrassing decisions. She found a hair dryer and completed the miracle, fluffing up the golden tresses for bedtime. Culley watched, his mind in turmoil.

"I'll turn in now if you don't mind," she said brightly. "I'm dog tired. It was nice of you to let me stay, Tom – I'm not much good on my own." She climbed into bed like an obedient child and was asleep almost immediately.

Culley doused the lights and got undressed, determined to have it out with the bloody woman first thing. He slept badly, with successive anxieties about (i) the criminal violence Kim assured him lay at Turner's fingertips, (ii) the business of her false passport and (iii) the whereabouts of the elusive Gordon woman toting the stolen organiser around Italy – all circling his brain like a manic roundabout. Eventually he did doze off, waking to the sound of more water flushing in the bathroom as the girl sluiced herself down again. She emerged fully dressed, the luminous skin faintly polished, tousled hair framing her face in a cloud. She made him a cup of tea, smiling as he rejected the long-life milk, chattering away like a magpie.

"Look, Kim, let's get one thing straight. I'm a policeman. It's impossible for me to condone any illegal activity you and your boyfriend have got yourselves into. That passport of yours, for instance. Martha Ferrero?"

She flopped on to the other bed watching him from under her lashes, clearly weighing up the likelihood of even seeing her new lover again.

"Andy got it for me. In case I needed to disappear. Raymond used to send me abroad to make arrangements about his numbered accounts. The Cayman Islands, Geneva sometimes. No big deal. But Andy thought I might find myself in a tight spot, need to make a quick getaway."

"Not Andy *Bailey* – not that twerp in the show flat?"

Kimberley bridled, jabbing at him to emphasise her point.

"Andy's been good to me. He just got cold feet, that's all – and who can blame him, poor duck, with people like Raymond stamping round?"

Culley gasped. "You can't be serious! Andy *Bailey* the new man in your life? Kimberley, you're having me on."

He leapt out of bed, stubbing his toe, yelped and made a grab at his underpants on the chair.

She shrugged. "You don't know him. He's absolutely brilliant in bed, believe me."

Culley limped round the room snatching up his clothes, and disappeared into the bathroom, fairly sizzling with irritation. Andy Bailey! That ponce. How could Kimberley fall for that line? And what sort of circles was Turner's salesman into where Swiss passports were on tap? She must be lying, covering up for her boss. Getting angry with the girl wasn't going to get him anywhere. Kimberley Carter was the only lead he'd got and falling out with her would scupper the whole sodding operation.

He emerged from the shower determined to face it out. In his absence she had phoned down for breakfast to be sent up, ordering a full range of continental goodies including cheese, fruit, croissants and an enormous pot of fragrant coffee. He grinned, deciding to play up his role and moving across to peck her cheek. "Sorry, sweetie. Jealousy I guess."

She looked pretty pleased with herself after that, doing all the hostessy bits with the plates and cups, passing him a napkin, pouring the coffee.

"What about your luggage?"

"Forget it. It's safe enough till I need it. I'll buy some fresh stuff when we get to Lucca."

"Lucca?"

"The Barclayson's place – it's near Lucca. It's not such a long drive. You'll love it."

"Why won't you go back to the hotel for your luggage?"

"I'm booked in as Carter – I don't want Raymond tracking me down – I'm safe here."

"That's why you bolted from the Danieli, isn't it?"

"The travel agent probably told him where I was. It was stupid of me not to think of it before. I shall just have to keep on the move till I catch up with Anabel Gordon. If I can recover his bloody organiser, if all else fails Raymond would forgive me, take me back like we were before."

Culley could believe it.

"Did you really think Andy Bailey was brave enough to throw up a cushy number with Turner to play house with you in the States?"

She sobered, sipping her orange juice, averting her eyes. "You don't know Andy. He's got balls all right. Just got worried when the Gordon girl got in the middle. Three's a crowd he said. Like Raymond he thought it was Abigail Griffith at first."

"I have met this guy, you know. Only once I admit. But he never struck me as any sort of a match for Raymond Turner. Anyway he reckoned he was on to a good thing there. Said Turner was about to appoint him to the board."

She looked up, utterly astonished. "Andy said that?"

He nodded. "He wasn't very complimentary about you either," he ventured, jabbing the poor girl where it hurt.

She gave a nervous laugh and stabbed at her croissant as if she meant it. "That was just cover. We had to be very careful. Raymond may have suspected I was cheating on him but he never, in a million years, considered Andy any sort of threat."

"Why did Andy want the organiser?"

She sighed, speaking patiently as if repeating a very boring story.

"It had all Raymond's contacts, his deals, dates, names, figures, everything. Andy wanted to take it over, to leapfrog Raymond's operation. Raymond's getting old and careless. Andy reckoned he could double the turnover in less than a year. Or, if necessary, go legit and take over the Development Company as chief executive."

"And risk Turner's bully boys? You realise we're talking money laundering here, Kim."

"With the organiser in his pocket Andy could either take over the money shifting lark or blow Raymond sky high – play the good guy and expose his rotten deals to the press, go public and get a medal for it from the establishment even if he couldn't take over the organiser business. The shareholders would back Andy all the way if Raymond got jailed. If I can get the organiser back *I'll* be the one calling the shots."

Culley whistled, convinced at last that Kimberley Carter actually knew what she was talking about. In retrospect the only valid piece of information Andy Bailey had shared with him was true: Kimberley Carter was no airhead.

"Do you think Andy still loves you?"

"Of course he does. We're a team. He's just playing possum till I get the organiser back. I told Andy I knew where it was before I flew out."

"The house on the *calle*? But she's scarpered, Kim. Anabel Gordon could be anywhere."

"She doesn't suspect me. Why should she? I don't mean her any harm, I just need to collect the rest of my stuff. I can't phone Andy at work and his mobile's on the blink for some reason but as soon as we get back from Lucca I'll wait for him here in Venice – leave a message at American Express so he knows where to find me then we can decide what to do."

"You seem so sure Gordon's on the level."

"*She* doesn't know what she's sitting on," she retorted. "Our first impression was wrong. She wasn't trying to blackmail me, just squeeze a decent bonus for returning my passports and the dollar bills. Andy thinks she's holding out on us, that she knows the real value of the organiser. But he's wrong. It was the Ferrero passport she thought I was paranoid about."

"What makes you so sure? She's certainly playing hide and seek extremely effectively. You don't even know what the cost is likely to be, do you, Kimberley?"

"She's not that bright, Tom. Nobody could be as fanciable as she is and yet be so skint. She was willing to play delivery girl for a measly reward. I'll just ring that Venice number again before we go, make sure she's not still in Tuscany."

Culley recoiled, seeing the hard edge of the beautiful facade. The girl was a complicated combination of childish greed, egomania and intuition. An explosive mix.

She stacked the plates and checked her tiny bag. "I need more cash. Can you bankroll our little excursion to Barclayson's place? I'll pay you back, Tom, I promise. I always cover my debts."

Culley picked up his jacket and took her arm, smiling thinly at the Manager as they made their way out into the square. Everywhere bells were tolling, the clangour reverberating in his brain like a death knell.

Twenty-Three

It was, as Kim had promised, a wonderful drive, sunshine slanting off rosy pantiles, a scent of wild honeysuckle blowing in the breeze. They took turns at the wheel, diverted by several wrong turnings in the clotted lanes south of the plain, eventually drawing up at La Colomba's big iron gates as the moon was rising.

It was quite a place. Even Kimberley was impressed. It did, however, strike a sombre note: there were no staff in evidence, no cars parked in the forecourt. Culley contented himself with the thought that even if they were on a fool's errand here he had at least got the Carter girl out of his hotel room and if Anabel Gordon was lurking in this wonderous castello, Kim's hunch had paid off.

As they slammed the doors of the little Fiat a rugger type with straw-coloured hair emerged from the darkness of the loggia, smiling cheerfully, presumably a member of Philip Barclayson's household, another art buff. Culley was a redneck when it came to art, especially the sort of stuff Kimberley asserted was Barclayson's speciality.

"The old fart can give the thumbs down on a canvas and its value instantly plummets," she had said. "The auction houses and dealers trust his judgement but I'm not so sure." Culley wondered where this cockney waif got so clued up on the

171

art front but he was in no position to argue and flexed his shoulders, stiff after the long drive, holding out his hand to the man who was greeting them.

"Hi! My name's Randall, Matt Randall. You a friend of Alys's? She's away in Rome for a few days. Staying with Professor Mortensen." The name dropping fell on deaf ears as far as Culley was concerned but Kimberley looked impressed. They shook hands, introducing themselves all round.

"Actually, we were hoping to catch Anabel," Culley said.

"Annie Gordon? Sorry, she's in London. Be back Wednesday. There's only me here, I'm afraid, but you're welcome to stay for supper. I could do with the company, folks." He led them through to the great hall, a Valhalla with windows presumably overlooking the surrounding hills. Kimberley looked suspicious, lips pouting like a spoilt brat. Matt poured the wine, unperturbed, and they awkwardly seated themselves before a magnificent log fire, the sort which could do service for an ox roast if called upon. Once the sun had gone the stone walls of the villa cooled, the vast rooms and passages taking on Gothic shadows.

"Anabel had to scoot – a family emergency."

"Will she be coming back here?"

"Sadly, no. She's working on a portrait at Alys's place. Venice. I can give you the address if you like."

"What cropped up?" Kimberley persisted.

"Her sister died. An overdose."

"Suicide?"

"Apparently not. The sister dabbled in drugs for years it seems. Had taken three overdoses before. Anabel thought she would pull through like the other times but it was too late. Alys phoned her in London, got the lowdown. Technically a mixture of methadone, valium and nitrazepam." He shrugged. "There was nothing anyone could do. Anabel's flying straight back after the funeral, says she prefers to bury herself in her work. A tragedy like that – her only relative – would be the only thing to drag that girl away from an important commission. You two known her long?"

Culley shook his head. "As a matter of fact I've never met her. But Kim needs to collect some personal items Anabel's been keeping till we got here."

"Sorry. A wasted journey. She was here for a while. Bad timing."

"But she's definitely coming back Wednesday," Kim interjected.

"Absolutely! Assured Alys she had almost finished this portrait for Philip and wanted to close the deal."

Kimberley relaxed, drifting off in a private reverie while the two men broke away from the Anabel theme and ranged over the delights of Tuscan architecture. A middle-aged woman appeared, addressing herself to Matt in rapid Italian, and after a brief exchange he turned to his guests, insisting they stay overnight.

"The rooms are always prepared for unexpected visitors, students and art freaks like me. Philip has a formidable reputation for open house. He would never forgive me if I turned you out into the night. Donatella will have supper ready in half an hour. I'll show you to your rooms. Would you like a lightning tour of La Colomba? It's a miracle of sympathetic restoration."

Kimberley stirred herself and they meandered through the long gallery to a magnificent dining room and then on to the library via a small anteroom which Matt described as Alys's centre of operations. Her study was a pretty room, the windows shuttered, an antique carved table set with a computer, two telephones and a stack of files. The petals from a vase of roses had scattered over Alys's papers, settling on to a heap of labelled keys tossed into a bowl. The men moved off to admire the adjoining library, Matt describing his research, laughter bouncing off the fuzzy murals, a repetitive grid pattern of fleur-de-lys in faded golds and greens on a blue ground. Kimberley remained in the more feminine anteroom soundlessly moving across the stone flags, delicately touching Alys's pretty things, sifting the rose petals through her fingers.

After supper she made her excuses and retired early, a girl with small reserves of stamina fatigued by the long drive. The men settled in the library with their cigarettes and coffee, hitting it off immediately.

Under the Canadian's persistent questioning, Culley admitted to being a policeman and his interest in Anabel Gordon part of an ongoing investigation. He produced his warrant card as if to convince his new friend of his credentials, sketching in the outline of the unsolved murder of Anabel's colleague, skipping the more brutal details, omitting all mention of the cigarette burns, the sadistic overtones of the crime scene something he preferred to gloss over. Matt grew pensive, mulling over something which clearly troubled him as he took it all in.

"What's Kimberley's angle?" he said at last.

"Not sure. Certainly at the margin of international crime of some sort."

"Art fraud?"

Culley looked up. "No, I don't think so though the girl can surprise you. Don't be taken in by the bimbo image – Kim's into something serious but I have to give her enough rope to bring the rest of the team down."

"She's involved in the murder?"

"Only indirectly. Might prove a useful witness if I can pin down some real evidence. The men she's in with are big players."

"Mafia?"

"By association, possibly." Culley's hands opened in a gesture of defeat. "Believe me, Matt, I'm working in the dark here. I'm not even officially on the case. I've taken leave to satisfy my own conscience – so many people are in danger here, not least your friend Anabel. How well do you know her?"

"Hardly at all. My role here is genuine enough. I am researching a book on Anthony Blunt, a Janus in the olympic class, but I've also been taking Judas money to get behind an art scam which Barclayson's allegedly at the heart of."

"Who brought you in?"

"Strictly between the two of us it was another connoisseur. A man called Royd-Chiddingstone, a big shot in the art game but an honest broker. He's been alarmed at the number of so-called mistakes auction houses have been tripped up by. Museum archives have been tampered with which doesn't help – provenances have been faked and sorting out the trumped up records could take years. Big money's involved and the people drawn to art as an investment are getting jittery. It could ruin a billion-dollar market in London."

"Dangerous?"

"Lethal."

"And Anabel Gordon may be caught up in this racket?"

"I hope not. The kid's not in the same league as these people, but who knows? What is she holding on to that Kimberley's so keen to retrieve?"

Culley described the disaster which had thrown the two girls together and explored the significance of the missing organiser.

Matt looked confused as well he might, the distance between the riders in this wall of death circuit closing in. He tried to fill in the blanks for this co-conspirator who had turned up out of the blue.

"Barclayson authenticates art works in private houses – he has his finger on nearly every desirable treasure in Britain. Exporting is ringed with problems but the old wolf is in a position not only to pinpoint the location of hundreds of paintings but the vulnerability of their security. Living for so many years in Italy I can only conclude he has the protection of the Family which makes me suspicious. To have remained untouched here, his home a no-go area despite the undisputed value of his collection, not to mention the wealthy guests who stay here untroubled by kidnapping or threats."

"Surely this region's not dangerous? It's hardly Sicily."

"Of course not. But it is a miracle you must admit. Barclayson keeps just one bodyguard who travels with him and the villa remains virtually unprotected when he's on one of his forays to New York or Paris."

Tom frowned. "Do you think Anabel Gordon's playing a double game? Got to hear about an impending art theft while she was in London? In a position to blow the whistle? Violence seems to be following her like a shadow. First her friend Griffith is tortured to extract information, then her sister dies in suspicious circumstances."

"And the fire. Don't forget the fire. Was she a target there?"

"Nobody knew she was at Zelini's that night – not even the police till later. She escaped by the skin of her teeth, threw herself from a first-floor window apparently – her doctor confirms that but there's no evidence of fire raising and the woman who was killed was an innocent bystander. Found dead in a toilet."

"Did she look like Annie?"

"What?"

"The woman who was trapped in the toilet."

Culley's jaw dropped. "Yes, as a matter of fact there was a striking resemblance – caused a bit of a mix-up to start with. But you're way off beam there, Matt. Smothering the victim backstage and then setting fire to a building full of customers is pretty far-fetched."

"Clever though if you could pull it off. Say someone dragged this poor woman into the cubicle and rendered her unconscious before starting the fire. Bet your forensic boys didn't think of that one!"

Culley jeered outright, slapping his thigh. Matt raised both hands in surrender. "OK, you're the expert. Just airing my socks. Hey, we're both winging it here, buddy. What's your plan for tomorrow?"

"If Anabel's stuck in London till after the funeral on Wednesday we might as well stay here if that's all right with you? When does Alys Trimmer get back?"

"At the weekend. Alys is OK. Sure, stick around, see which way the wind blows."

"Just so long as I keep close to Kimberley I won't miss any action."

"You involved with this chick?"

"Sexually? Well, no, since you ask. Been tempted – who wouldn't be? But there's something off-key there. Now you see it, now you don't. First off she's all tears, needs protecting, appeals to my big manly ego. Next, in a blink, the golden angel's vaporised. Kimberley Carter's merely the stuff of wet dreams, take my word for it, probably break your neck if you tried to get a leg over."

The following day Culley's angel did disappear. Said she

was driving into town to do some sightseeing, refused to let Tom along for the ride. But when the cool dusk closed in and Kimberley and the hire car were still missing, the two men dismally concluded that they had been given the slip.

But they were wrong.

Twenty-Four

Kimberley strolled back into the drawing room at the point where, after a couple of bottles of wine, they were planning to hire a new car for Culley to return to Venice next morning. They shot out of their seats, temporarily speechless. Kimberley grinned, posing in the doorway wearing a new dress, twirling in the candlelight like the fairy on the Christmas tree.

"Where've you been?" Tom barked.

"Shopping, of course. I told you."

"You've been gone all day!"

"So?"

"So we were worried. Anyway, I thought you hadn't got any money on you?"

"You're not the only man in this bloody place. I bet you thought I'd pinched your horrible little hire car, didn't you, Tom?" She helped herself to some wine and lit a cigarette, perching on the arm of Matt's chair and ruffling his hair.

Culley turned away. "Of course not. But you could have phoned."

"Why? You two boys not big enough to play on your own for a couple of hours?"

Donatella broke up the spat by coming in to announce

179

dinner and the three of them trooped into the dining room, the atmosphere tense.

But Matt's natural ebullience combined with Kim's over-riding *joie de vivre* lubricated by more wine from the cellar eventually won over Culley's sulks. By midnight Kim had decided they must try out the swimming pool and the noisy threesome were as one, not least because skinny-dipping under the stars to the accompaniment of a mournful barn owl made everything else seem irrelevant.

Next morning Kimberley rose late, joining Matt in the library where he was working through a pile of old corre-spondence from Philip's files. Kim had changed into jeans and a silk T-shirt, her long hair in a ponytail, her mood unsinkably buoyant. She teased Matt into giving her a tour of the estate, dragging him away from his dusty records, cutting Tom dead when he appeared from the garden. Matt shrugged incomprehensibly as he passed, as puzzled as Culley by the girl's capriciousness.

After lunch Tom heard the car start in the yard and ran out, stepping in front of the Fiat as Kimberley attempted to drive off. The engine stalled and she swore, trying to accelerate away as he dragged open the door and jumped in. Furious, she switched off, bawling at him in none too fragrant terms to get out. He braced himself against her blows, implacable, ignoring her outrage. At last, breathing heavily, she gave in.

"OK. If you want to play it like a bloody duet be my guest. I'm only getting my fuckin' hair done, for Christ's sake. I made the appointment yesterday – I haven't time to argue the toss!"

"A hairdo? In Lucca?" Culley was genuinely taken aback but as they drove through the leafy lanes his humour got the better of him and he grinned to himself, realising all too clearly that getting a blow-dry was just the sort of business that a girl like Kimberley *would* give priority to.

He glanced at the milometer. At a rough estimate she had been ranging further afield than Lucca on yesterday's shopping expedition. He spoke in glowing terms of her new designer jeans and Armani T-shirt and she relaxed, expertly speeding round the narrow lanes, a girl clearly not only familiar with the region but a driver of considerable style.

"Where did you go?" he said evenly.

"I told you. Sightseeing."

"Not in Lucca."

"Buzzed off to Pisa, didn't I? Wanted to see that old tower they've got there. Fantastic. Flopping sideways like poor old Raymond's willy." She giggled, high as a kite. It struck Culley that the girl had shopped for more than a change of clothing during all those missing hours away from La Colomba. He hoped they would get back before her marching powder wore off. He slid down in the passenger seat, relieved when she slowed down outside a salon on a side street within spitting distance of the Lucca bus terminus. She stood on the pavement gesturing towards an information centre for tourists off the square, her ponytail swirling in the wind like a skein of yellow silk.

"I'll meet you over there at four o'clock. OK? You can sit and watch the car all afternoon if you like but I'm going nowhere till tomorrow. Then we'll drive back to Venice and wait for Anabel, shall we?" Her tone was sarcastic but he let it go, testing his policeman's vibes to the limit.

"Can I trust you?"

She laughed. "If you'd brought your handcuffs, Sergeant, we could have sat under the dryer together. Kinky, eh?" She sobered. "Don't be a chump, Tommy. Where would I go? Just be here at four – I shan't wait. If you're late you'll just have to walk all the way home, won't you? You can get a map of the town over there. They've got all the tourist stuff. Relax. Take in the sights. Enjoy yourself for a change, you old misery."

"Hand over the car keys."

She grinned and blew him a kiss as she disappeared into the salon. Culley sighed, knowing himself to be outclassed with girls like Kimberley Carter. And Gerry. And probably Anabel Gordon too if he was honest.

He took her advice and got some leaflets from the information centre, filling in the afternoon with a tour of the medieval streets.

At four o'clock, good as her word, the Fiat drew into the kerb beside him. At first Culley stepped back, momentarily off balance. It was Kim all right but almost unrecognisable. She wound down the window and smiled, wrinkling her nose under the dark sunglasses, tickled pink by his surprise. Drawing on her cigarette, she shook out her new hairstyle. The blonde tresses had been sheared to a geometric bob like a Japanese doll. Except the colour was now fiercely auburn, burning bright. The girl looked utterly different, only the little heart-shaped mole at the corner of her mouth stamping her identity.

"Don't you like it?" she said, all smiles, cute as an alley cat.

Culley gulped. "Sure. But I liked it before."

"Old stick-in-the-mud."

Let's go round the corner so I can get used to it. Have a drink. There's a nice little bar I spotted." He tried to open the door to let her out but it was locked. He gripped the edge of the glass, suddenly wary, and in a flash her hand snaked out and she stubbed her cigarette on his hand. He yelped, leaping back, stung.

"Hey!"

"Here. Put these back in Alys's bowl, will you?" She dropped a bunch of keys into the gutter and swiftly wound up the window to within a few inches. "We don't want her to think we've been snooping, do we? Sorry, Tom, but I've gotta go. I'll return the car to the hire place at the airport. I'm splitting. Ciao."

And before he had the chance to react she had driven off. He sucked at the cigarette burn on the back of his hand, mad as hell. The keys lay in the wet gutter the label smudging in the outflow from a drainpipe on the wall. He snatched them up, feeling as if he had been mugged on the street. The label bore Alys's firm script: they were her spare keys for the apartment in Venice.

Twenty-Five

By the time he had found a taxi to take him back to La Colomba it was too late to pursue her.

He stormed into her quarters, Matt at his heels, guessing that the cunning wretch had pulled yet another fast one on Culley. The drawers had been emptied, even the yellow dress she had travelled down in whisked away. Matt pulled him out and Tom stumped back downstairs to the library to vent his impotent fury on his hapless listener.

"She dumped me, Matt! Left me at the roadside like some fucking hitchhiker. And it was *my* car, dammit."

"Obviously had it all planned – probably stashed all her stuff into the car after our swim last night. There was something. I should have mentioned it to you before but it seemed pretty sneaky. Kim made a lot of phonecalls very early this morning. It woke me. Hearing her muffled voice from the next room, I picked up my bedside extension."

"Catch anything?"

Ruefully Matt admitted listening in on the fag end of one of her calls before decency got the better of him. "Some bloke, English I think . . ."

"Who?"

"Didn't catch his name but Kim said she'd see him at the airport."

"Where?"

"She didn't say."

Culley thumped the table. "Shit! He didn't call her Martha by any chance?"

"Sorry?"

"She has another passport. In the name of Martha Ferrero. And I haven't even told you the bit about the hairdo yet!"

Matt listened patiently while Culley vented his spleen on the bolter, describing the new-look Kimberley/Martha with relish.

"A redhead? Sure it wasn't a wig?"

Culley stopped short. "Possibly. But I was within a foot of her as she sat in the car. It didn't look like a wig to me. Is it important? Obviously she's doing a flit. But where?"

"She admitted going to Pisa yesterday. She could have been booking a flight out."

"Back to London? If she was phoning Raymond Turner this morning that would be the next move. But why disguise herself?"

Matt poured a stiff whisky for himself and Culley nodded, accepting a second glass, his ego in shreds.

"And what was she doing with Alys's keys?" he said, producing the labelled set from his pocket and handing them over.

Matt scrutinised the keys and Alys's handwriting. "They're the originals all right. If Kim's going home she's clearly had second thoughts about confronting Anabel before she goes back. Maybe she's making a clean break from all her old haunts and ditching Turner altogether."

"But why borrow the keys?"

"To get copies cut? She was gone all day yesterday, had all the time in the world to fix it."

"But why go to all that trouble? If she wanted to search Anabel's flat before she gets back why not just take the originals? We hadn't missed them and Alys isn't due here for days by which time the girl could be anywhere."

"Didn't she drop so much as a hint about her plans, Tom?"

"She was banking on her new boyfriend, Andy Bailey, joining her in Venice last weekend but he never showed up. She was even considering going back to Turner, appealing to the poor sap to take her back but whatever way she jumps the organiser would be a useful bargaining chip."

"Unless she means to dump both Turner and the new guy."

"Go it alone? Possible – and she could have access to Turner's numbered Swiss bank accounts not to mention his 'wandering funds'."

Matt whistled, putting the keys aside while the two tried to second-guess Kim's next move.

"My bet is Anabel flew to her sister's deathbed in such a panic she left all Kim's stuff at Alys's flat."

"She doesn't know what she's sitting on according to Kim. She reckoned Anabel would have no qualms about handing over the organiser so long as she got the reward she had been promised."

"And no alarm bells are ringing? Even after the Griffith murder? Anabel's no fool, Tom. I've met her, remember."

"As far as I know she had no reason to connect Griffith with Kimberley Carter."

"Well, if Kim thinks she can sweet-talk Annie into handing over the stuff without any trouble, even to someone acting on her behalf, and if Anabel's due back in Venice tomorrow night you had better get your skates on and warn her."

"I'll hire another car."

"No need. We'll go together. Perhaps, if we try really hard, the two of us together might manage to outwit one blonde," Matt cynically commented.

"One redhead."

They laughed, content that at least they had some sort of cockeyed plan on the table.

Matt spent the evening packing up his typed notes and photocopying a whole lot of data from Barclayson's files.

Culley watched him from the doorway. "You finished here?"

"Got all I need." He glanced up, suddenly looking older as if the grim shadows of La Colomba had gathered a burden of troubles about his formerly carefree existence. They ate in style that night, Donatella's obvious reluctance to see her nice young men back on the road warming their departure.

"I telephoned Alys," Matt said. "Told her I'd be in Venice for a while and would be in touch."

They took the trip at a leisurely pace, stopping off for lunch, knowing Anabel's arrival back at the flat was not scheduled till eight at the earliest. Matt was bunking down with a colleague out near the Ghetto, promising to meet up with Culley for dinner at the bistro on the opposite corner to Anabel's flat.

Tom was waiting with a bottle of wine and they sat in the soft evening air waiting for the lights to go on on the upper floor of Alys's building. When eleven o'clock chimed and there still seemed no reoccupation Culley grew nervous, sensing yet another sleight of hand at Kimberley's instigation. Matt suggested they tried to get a glimpse of the back windows via the scrappy area at the rear, and they sauntered to the next *calle* spotting a partial collapse of the end wall that feral cats used as an entry to the so-called gardens.

Matt stood guard while Culley squeezed through, passers-by

incurious after a night out on the town. Strings of washing flapped high overhead, strung between the buildings, accessed from the balconies by a convenient pulley system. It took Tom several minutes to negotiate the piles of rubbish and broken pots which littered the yard but at last he managed to get a look at the upper windows. Sure enough the shutters to Alys's flat remained unsecured, an overhead light on the top floor shining weakly into the night. He waited, hoping to see Anabel and possibly Kim cross his line of vision but the shadow which periodically shut off his view of the room was blurred. It was, however, without a doubt the bulky outline of a man.

He scrambled back through the broken wall and held a whispered conference with Matt.

"There's someone up there with her. A man. They must have closed the front curtains or something. I'll knock and see if she'll come down."

Matt shook his head. "That won't work. If you want to find out what's going on you've got to barge straight in and catch them before the guy has a chance to hide. Who do you think it is?"

"If Kim's alerted Turner, told him the actual whereabouts of his money laundering records, I'd put my bet on Turner coming to Italy himself – just to make sure Kimberley isn't double-crossing him again."

"They must have been up there for hours. We couldn't miss seeing anyone approach the front door from where we were sitting, could we? Maybe it's just a friend of Annie's."

"And maybe it's Turner. But he knows me. He won't want to cause trouble with a policeman who can put the finger on him afterwards."

"Kim might be up there with them, you realise. For all you know she's fed Turner the line that you're as bent as everyone else. Came here on a private excursion to grab the organiser for yourself. A huge blackmailing tool in anyone's hands."

"Oh, shut up, Matt! I've got enough worries without your dismal weather forecasts. Just wait here."

Matt thrust something into his hand as Culley was about to move away. The keys.

"Just drop in on them. I'll be at the cafe over there in case you need cavalry reinforcements." Matt slapped him on the shoulder, his smile forced.

Culley nodded and crossed to the shabby entrance and disappeared inside without a sound, leaving the door slightly ajar. Matt positioned himself at a table on the other side of the alley where he could watch for any movements upstairs.

Culley crept up the unlit stairway, straining to hear sounds from the upper floor. It wasn't until he had silently turned the key in Anabel's front door that voices percolated from the inner room. Only one overhead bulb lit the tableau, the feeble illumination throwing the scene into stark relief.

Facing Culley as he peered round the door was Anabel Gordon tied to an upright chair, her fuzz of dark hair just as he had imagined it, her eyes closed. Blood from a gaping wound in her neck had stained her shirt which had been pulled open exposing her breasts. Culley had come too late.

The man silhouetted against the light was smoking a cigarette, speaking softly as he, with slow deliberation, slashed at a portrait of a young girl propped up on an easel. Culley relived in his inflamed imagination the memory of Abigail Griffith tied up in her bathroom, and before he had a chance to make a coherent plan of attack, anger surged and, uttering a piercing yell, he flung himself at the man's back.

Anabel's attacker lurched under Culley's surprise assault and stumbled to his knees, the knife skittering across the floor. The girl screamed, revived from her pain, as the two threw wild blows at each other like madmen.

Culley straddled his opponent, a lucky left hook rendering him temporarily senseless. He lay on the rug, blood gushing from his mouth, and Tom turned towards the girl. As he attempted to untie her the man reared up behind him, bunched fists crashing into the nape of his neck like a hammer blow. Culley buckled, seeing stars, falling against Anabel's chair and causing it to topple over, the girl still pinioned.

He blacked out for a second and when he came to Andy Bailey was gone, only his footsteps to be heard beating a retreat into the street below. The door banged behind him, echoing in the stairwell like the last trump. Culley tried to raise himself but collapsed again, hitting his head an unnecessary knock-out blow on the stove in the corner of the room. The girl's screams reverberated through the empty building, bloodcurdling, loud enough to raise the dead.

But nobody came.

Twenty-Six

P eople did come, of course. Eventually.

But her screams were masked by the uproar in the street below as Matt flew from his seat outside the cafe to give chase to Bailey, a waiter, shouting obscenities, in close pursuit. The three men grappled like all-in wrestlers, the Italian bawling for the onlookers to call the police, a small crowd jeering encouragement to the Englishmen, presumably football hooligans slogging it out in a running battle.

It was only when the police joined in and forcibly broke it up that the bloodied combatants were finally parted, the Italian repeating his charge that "the fair-haired bruiser had skipped without paying the bill." Matt and Bailey were swiftly hauled off to the *questura*, only Matt's fluent Italian preventing them both from being thrown into the cooler overnight. Bailey said nothing, gingerly exploring his mouth and spitting out a tooth. After intensive argument the guard was eventually persuaded to call out the *commissario* who arrived, considerably aggrieved, to unknit the apparently simple problem of a drunken brawl.

It took nearly an hour for Matt to convince the *commissario* and only after threats to call in diplomatic support was a patrol sent back to the scene of the fracas to investigate the Canadian's claims of a serious incident having taken place on the top floor of an apparently empty building. It would be necessary to break in, that was the trouble, thus calling into play requirements of an official nature. Luckily when Matt was allowed to accompany them to the door an elderly woman leaned out of a window in the adjoining house to complain to the police about domestic violence in the next door flat, the racket having seriously interrupted her viewing of the lottery results.

Having paid off the waiter with sincere apologies Matt now insisted on paying for any damage to the door if they could please stop fucking about and do their job. He was swiftly handcuffed to a young officer and dragged back to the launch. To be fair, once given the all clear by the furious *commissario*, two elegantly uniformed muscle men attacked the antique door with enthusiasm.

They were almost too late, Anabel's considerable loss of blood rendering her unconscious alongside an apparent corpse. They untrussed her from the chair and while waiting for the emergency services applied themselves to Culley. He came round as they manhandled him down the stairs, his feeble words, "The girl?" meeting only blank faces. *"La signorina?"* he repeated with growing alarm as they lifted him into the launch. His head felt like the football booted about in a World Cup Final and it was only when an English-speaking doctor got to hear the full story that Matt was allowed out of the cells and Bailey put on a charge.

In fact, Culley's injuries were far from life-threatening; Matt himself sported an impressive black eye when he came to collect him from hospital and whisked him to the private clinic to which Philip Barclayson had generously transferred Anabel as soon as he heard of the assault. They had permission for a very short visit.

"Bailey's still locked up, please God?" Culley demanded.

"Absolutely! And your boss from England's been flown in, Superintendent Ackroyd, to clarify the investigation."

"Really? I'd like to see the *commissario*'s efforts to co-ordinate enquiries with that old bastard."

They were admitted to Anabel's room with a pass, Culley relieved to see a police guard posted outside her door. Was she still at risk?

She greeted her two saviours with curiosity, one she had never met before and Matt, merely a passing acquaintance, who, the commissario assured her, had saved her life. Matt introduced Culley and dragged chairs to the bedside, anxious to hear the full story though they'd been warned they must not tire her. After twenty-four hours on a drip Anabel still looked pale as a Botticelli angel, her neck swathed in bandages and three fingers in splints.

"Matt, I can't begin to thank you," she muttered, her voice hoarse and barely audible.

"Tom here's the hero. My only claim to a medal was to persuade a bunch of Italian policemen that I wasn't a drunken oaf who'd tried to run off without paying for the drinks."

"Look Anabel, we can't stay long – the doctor was reluctant to allow us in here at all. But I need to know what happened. For my report," he added, far from certain what view Ackroyd would take of his dubious interference in a CID investigation he had been warned, several times, to keep his nose out of. She looked down at her hands folded on the sheet, reliving the painful incident as she spoke.

"OK. Well, I got back at seven. Caught an earlier plane – you know about my sister's funeral?"

Matt nodded, patting her hand.

"It wasn't until I got inside the flat and had closed the door I realised that Andy Bailey was waiting."

"He had keys?"

"Kimberley had given him duplicates she'd got from somewhere. She met him at Pisa airport on Monday. He seemed anxious to put the record straight. They were in it together at first but she got scared, told him she wanted out."

"Kim's gone back to London?"

"No. 'Gone underground' was the way he put it."

"Sounds quite a conversation."

"I was in no position to argue. He caught me unawares, was standing behind the door, I suppose. Hadn't intended to hang around he said, thought he could find what he was looking for before I got back. He'd certainly turned over poor Alys's place."

"He attacked you?"

"Not at first. At first he was very polite. Said I had something of Kimberley's and I was to hand it over because he had to get back to London on the first available plane."

"Why didn't you just give the organiser to him straight off?"

"It was something he said about Abigail, a casual aside in passing. Sympathised with me, knowing, he said, that she was a friend of mine. He said it was appalling her being tortured like that. Cigarette burns – barbaric, he said. Something clicked. No wonder Kimberley got scared – I think she smelt danger. No-one had even mentioned cigarette burns – there was nothing in the press about that. While I was back in England for Ronnie's funeral I got a whole load of cuttings from an agency my boyfriend Solomon subscribes to. He knew I felt bad about not sending any flowers or anything and because I had been away when it happened I'd missed out on most of the news. I would have remembered any mention of cigarette burns – the rest of it was horrible enough." She reached across and poured a glass of water, her hand shaking.

"How did Andy know you and Abigail Griffith were friends?"

"I asked him that. He used to date a secretary in her office apparently. Daisy someone or other, works for the new art editor now he said."

"So he could have been familiar with Griffith's work routine, the frequency of bike messengers making emergency deliveries to her home at night."

"I suppose so." Anabel lay back on the pillows, closing her eyes in an effort to concentrate. Matt threw Culley a warning glance and tapped his watch, all too aware that their inquisition was draining her limited stamina. But Tom wouldn't let it go and after a sip of water, Anabel continued.

"At first Andy was polite, apologising for the break-in, excusing himself with lack of time before his plane left. Once he realised I was suspicious he stepped up the persuasion, throwing down a bundle of money and promising more. He looked such a berk, Matt, just one of thousands cloned in those private schools, totally unthreatening. Know what I mean? He was so out of place in Alys's flat, still neat in his pinstriped suit, the rooms shambolic around him. I almost felt sorry for the guy, still thought he was just the messenger boy, see, a harmless Hooray Henry. But that remark about the cigarette burns kept flickering at the back of my mind. I pretended I didn't know what he was talking about and told him I would only deal with Kimberley. That was my mistake."

She gulped, touching the bandages around her neck, clearly in pain. Culley urged her to go on, fiercely determined to have this chance.

"He suddenly flew at me. I wasn't expecting anything like *that*. He literally threw himself at me in a terrible rage. Talk about Jekyll and Hyde!"

"He knocked you down?" Matt's shiner seemed to emphasise his distress, his bloodshot eye burning like a beacon.

"Caught me off balance. Normally I'm quite nifty with my footwork but Andy had changed into a monster in a split second. Grabbed me by the hair and produced a length of rope from his pocket. Tightened it around my neck, threatening to strangle me. I went quietly after that, thinking I could talk him round, still unconvinced that he would actually kill me. There was no point in screaming for help – those old houses are solid and most of them are empty till after Easter anyway."

"Then he tied you to the chair?"

"At first I thought he was playing the fool, but he'd had quite a few drinks and was getting really nasty. We must have been alone up there for hours and I tried to keep him talking, tried to kid him I'd put the bloody book in a safe deposit in Venice while I was away for the funeral. He put me through the mincer with that stupid idea. I couldn't even come up with an address so that didn't wash, only made him even more mad with me. Andy *knew* I'd stashed the bloody thing somewhere in the flat. He'd been there the day before searching and he'd tried again the next evening hoping to get hold of it and be away before I got back – someone told him my plane was due Wednesday night, God knows how he found out."

"When did he start brandishing the knife?"

She closed her eyes again, her cheeks ashen. "Can't remember. He said he'd slash my painting, thought that'd fire me up. I laughed. That was the least of my worries. Bad move. He swung round and jabbed my throat, probably an accident but all that blood spurting out seemed to give him the hots. I still wouldn't give in – what could I lose by that stage? It was a one-way street and I knew it. Then he started breaking my fingers with a heavy candlestick, one by one, saying I'd never be able to hold so much as a pencil again."

She started to weep, impatiently brushing away the tears with her damaged hand. Matt half rose from his seat, pulling at Culley's sleeve, but Tom wouldn't give way and shrugged him off. After a minute Anabel continued, her voice now barely a whisper.

"He drank quite a lot after that and it was getting awfully dark in the room. I thought he might pass out but the man has the constitution of an ox. That's when he started rambling about taunting Abigail with his cigarette and it would be my turn next."

"He admitted that?"

"He insisted the other guy started it but any fool could see Andy was revelling in it like some sort of bloody S and M. weirdo. He tore open my shirt and said I'd better stop wasting his time. I knew then he was never going to let me walk away once I produced what he wanted, the longer I held out the more chance I had of seeing him crash out."

"Did he name the other guy?"

"Some sort of bouncer, Andy said. One of Turner's heavies he'd employed to keep an eye on Kimberley."

"Ah, the van driver," Culley breathed. "Did he say Turner had sent them to Griffith's flat to recover the organiser?"

"Definitely not. Andy was freelancing and cock-a-hoop with himself. Never taken a chance like this before, I guess. Even had Kimberley on a bit of string he said. He thought he needed Kim at first but then saw his big chance when Turner picked up on my initials and thought Abigail had been at Zelini's and was holding the stuff. He decided to go for it and realised he didn't need a partner after all, Kim was expendable once he'd tracked down the details. His new plan was to have it both ways – gain control over Turner at work and make him share the money-shifting profits at the same time. Once he had all Turner's secret files he could call the shots. Quite clever really, no need to turn Turner in and cause a stink which would be commercial suicide for the Corporation and lose the profits from the money racket. He planned to force Turner to take him on to the board, said he deserved it and Turner was pissing him around. Said he would eventually take control of the company now Kimberley was off the scene. All he needed was the book. I was crying, begging him to let me go but he'd gone too far – why would he let me live knowing everything like I did?"

"You're sure he hasn't harmed Kimberley?"

"No reason to. She wasn't a threat – she had too much to lose if she turned informer. She wanted out. Perhaps she suspected him of being in on the killing. Told him when she handed over the keys at the airport that she was going to disappear abroad, he said. Had plans of her own with a new partner. Where did *she* get keys for the flat anyway?"

"It's a long story. But, quick, before they turn us out. Where did you hide the organiser?"

She smiled, relaxing back on the pillows with a sigh.

"Ah. Well, that was the only clever move I made in my stupid runaround. I put it in a plastic bag inside a pillowcase and pegged it with safety pins on the washing line with my smalls. Pulleyed it out of reach with all the other laundry. Women here have always got stuff drying outside. I knew no-one would look out the window – not even Kimberley."

At that moment the door opened and Solomon Cheyney

crept in behind the biggest bunch of yellow roses Matt had ever seen outside a shop.

Anabel lit up, her face aglow.

"Isn't that just my luck?" she croaked. "I wait years for a good-looking man to appear and then three come along at once. Just like the number eleven bus."

Twenty-Seven

It was more than a month after he got back to London before
Culley thought to phone Marianne Butler and ask her out.
He took her to see a fringe company which was doing an all
male version of *Little Women* in drag. She took it in good
part and afterwards, downstairs in the bar, they sat down to
pub grub and a reconstruction of his Italian excursion.

Marianne looked very pretty in the candlelight. Gamine was
the word, what with her spiky hair and leggings.

"So your copyist has gone legit you reckon?" she said.

"Moved in with a gallery owner, Solomon Cheyney, and—"

"Solomon Cheyney! Wow."

"You've heard of him?"

"Who hasn't? One of the leading dealers in contemporary
British art, and sexy with it. Lucky girl. And Solomon's banned
the pastiche work?"

"He's funding Anabel to get out of the rat race. Now her
sister's no longer a drag on her finances she can do her
own thing, presumably. Don't ask me," he said, stroking
her hand which lay on the table, "I know sod all when it
comes to art."

"And your Canadian friend. Was he an undercover investi-
gator of this fraud scam?"

"In a small way. He warned the big guy involved and he's

retiring. No scandal but Matt's holding on to his evidence just in case."

"Great! These dealers peddling fakes should be lined up against a wall and shot," she said, vehemently attacking her bangers and mash. "What are the charges against this Bailey bloke?"

"In Italy everything you can think of bar kidnapping the Pope. Here, murder, with his accomplice on a lesser charge."

"OK. But when will he be brought back to stand trial?"

"He's still being held in Venice. The superintendent's trying to sort it out but the Italian paperwork's like a snowstorm. Actually, it's not all bad – it gives Ackroyd time to tie up the loose ends. Bailey refuses to admit exactly what he was doing in Abigail Griffith's flat and as far as anyone can work out, the other guy wasn't in on the secret. He was just there to add muscle."

"I thought that was the whole point. Bailey was after the money laundering data you said."

"Well, he was once he got on to Anabel and my bet is that was the target when he hit the Griffith place. But he refuses to admit as much and since I dropped a tip to Ackroyd that there was this government frontbencher who was involved with the dead woman there remains a remote possibility that—"

"A minister?" Marianne spluttered.

"Not exactly."

"Government sleaze. Whoops. Another man with his head on the block?" she chortled. "Why hasn't all this come out? Don't tell me political cover-ups are on your agenda now!"

"Marianne! For Christ's sake keep your voice down. It's still under investigation. Anyway, it wasn't a man so don't get your hopes up."

"A girly thing! You're telling me that poor art editor was tortured to give evidence against another woman?"

"Just forget I mentioned it. Ackroyd's all hot under the collar as it is and getting frigid responses from the top brass. He's hoping some tabloid tripe-hound will get wind of it and save us the embarrassment of airing it in public ourselves."

"Does your superintendent know the name of this woman on the front bench? And where do you fit in?"

"I was told in confidence and no, no-one has yet discovered who Griffith's womanfriend was or, if they have, they're not saying. The man who tipped me off is probably consulting his PR man as we speak, planning how to blow the scandal on to the front page to the highest bidder."

"But do you really think Bailey was on to it? Was trying to break down Abigail Griffith so he could sell the story himself?"

"No, I don't. Bailey didn't move in the right circles to pick up a scoop like that. I'm sticking to the supposition that the nasty little turd had only one idea and that was to rip off his boss, Raymond Turner."

"But you don't really know, do you?"

"Early days yet," Culley reluctantly admitted. "Something might turn up. And we've got the other guy, the van driver who was following Anabel's friend Kimberley. A small-time crook called Dicky Ray. He's willing to inform against Bailey so once we get him back here in the UK there should be a cast-iron case. We've also turned up Bailey's fingerprints at Anabel's old flat in Brixton which substantiates the case."

"What about the motorbike?"

"What motorbike?"

"I thought it said on the news when the story first broke that the police were searching for two bike messengers who were caught on the security video."

"But Bailey didn't need a bike. They drove up in the van according to Lee."

"You mean the accomplice was the bloke filmed at Griffith's entrance lobby?"

Culley sighed, elaborately spelling it out. "Marianne, my poppet. Are you sitting comfortably? Then I'll begin. Bailey didn't need a motorbike, he only needed to *look* like an express delivery guy and we found a biker's helmet in one of the cupboards at the show flat which might fit the bill."

"And it's Bailey's?"

"Ackroyd can't get *anyone* to admit owning it and, to a jury, Andy Bailey hardly looks as if he could be convincing as a man in leathers. He must have borrowed the gear from someone but Lee isn't saying."

"Phew! You have been a busy little sergeant, haven't you?"

Culley grinned. "Can't win 'em all though. Kimberley, the blonde I told you about, has vanished without a trace though Bailey did mention Argentina for what it's worth. And Raymond Turner's lawyers are likely to get Turner off scot-free. Without a statement from the blonde and because most of the data in the organiser is encoded there's very little proof which would hold up in court. Bailey has no insider information about the money laundering and Kimberley's done a flit so it looks as if Turner Developments are in the clear. The fraud lot are handling that side of it but you know what they're like – it could take years and at the end of the day an unsuccessful fraud trial is the last thing they want."

"Is a line out for Kimberley?"

"She hasn't really done anything worth an international

dragnet. She definitely wasn't involved in the Griffith killing, the van driver swears to that. Playing courier for Raymond Turner was dodgy but with her looks once she stands up in the dock swearing she was just an innocent messenger no jury on earth would convict her. It's really not worth pursuing."

"At least you caught Bailey. He wasn't so clever was he?"

"An ambitious thicko choked by his old school tie. Getting desperate. Seeing his chances slipping away and Raymond Turner promoting a cockney dumb blonde over his head was the last straw."

"Is Kimberley not bright then?"

"She's no dumb blonde. Believe me, Kimberley Carter's a very smart girl. She'll bob up again one of these days running her own corporation. She was more than a match for us and Turner will have to watch his back. She's on the loose and still has all the info about his numbered accounts and off-shore dealings. Let's hope she doesn't get too demanding and ends up on a slab like the Griffith woman, not that Turner had anything to do with that but he does have funny friends. There was one thing though. Do you remember me telling you about that very expensive bag of Kim's that started all this?"

"The crocodile job?"

"Yeah. Last thing Anabel said as I was leaving was, 'Will I have to give up the handbag?' "

"She wanted to *keep* it?"

"Said it was the only genuine article she'd ever had."

"But the police need it – for evidence or something?"

"I told her to tuck it away, say she'd lost it. Having been scarred for life by that freaker Bailey and getting her fingers broken, I thought walking away with a prize of a sort was the least she deserved."

Marianne looked puzzled. "Those big sloaney bags are for

old ladies. Why would a hip girl like Anabel Gordon want to cling on to it?"

"Like she said. It wasn't fake. As simple as that. A souvenir maybe." He paid the bill and pulled Marianne to her feet. "Enough of all that sad stuff, how about you coming back to my place for coffee? It's pretty sensational for a copper's pad I promise you."

"The wages of sin?"

He shrugged. "You could be right. My flat was the only thing I salvaged from my naughty ways as a City trader. Come on, Marianne, don't let your socialist ethics spoil the fun."

She laughed, dragging at her Guatemalan poncho as they ran for the bus.

When Kimberley decided to fly back to London to make her peace with Raymond Turner she didn't expect to wind up dead. Who would? Certainly not Superintendent Ackroyd, who had assumed that the Griffith murder and its cast list were all but wrapped up.

Twenty-Eight

Six weeks with Fernando in Chile was more than enough for Kimberley Carter. Out of context her latin lover had been sensational: on home ground his macho egocentricity made even Andy Bailey seem, in retrospect, mildly appealing.

The details of Andy's arrest in Venice percolated her sundrenched bolthole in snippets gleaned from the foreign papers. At first, being with Fernando in this strange place made the danger she had so narrowly escaped seem as utterly surreal as a side-effect of sunstroke. The brutality he had apparently inflicted on both the Griffith woman and Anabel seemed, at this distance, like some gothic melodrama, the identity of Andy Bailey upon which both the Italian and the British police were basing their prosecutions totally at variance with the man she had thought she knew.

Kimberley shared none of these troublesome anxieties with Fernando and with her new persona as Martha Ferrero Fernando, he remained blissfully unaware of the dark secrets his English dolly bird was harbouring.

Things started to go wrong right from the start. Firstly, he hated her new red-haired bob, the blond mane being paramount in his libido rating. And then, away from the chic London clubs where their secret liaison had flared simultaneously

206

with the Bailey love affair, Fernando's smart cookie lost a lot of her credibility, not helped by her non-existent Spanish. Also, Fernando's mother took against the girl, being especially critical of her fragile appearance. Most certainly not child-bearing hips.

Kimberley juggled her options and decided, on balance, Raymond Turner must come to her rescue. Within a month she began to ring him daily, wistfully pleading for his under-standing, begging the man to understand her stupid infatuation with Bailey who, it turns out, was a killer. Initially reluctant, the older man gradually thawed, assuming the silly girl's flight to Chile of all places was an understandable bid to escape any questioning from the police. In fact, going to ground like that was useful: the poor kid knew too much for her own good.

It was finally agreed she would fly back to Europe and cover the last leg of the journey by devious routes and hope that her British passport did not feature on any wanted list. Raymond promised to make discreet enquiries to see whether a warrant for her arrest was on hold which seemed unlikely at the present convoluted stages of investigation existing between the Italian and British teams.

She slipped back into Waterloo via the Channel tunnel, the fresh summer breeze like the very breath of life to her parched lungs. Raymond was waiting at home, a bottle of champagne chilled in readiness, his sheer stability a sure aphrodisiac to Kim after a rackety couple of months on the run.

He took her in his arms, stroking the boyish bronze cap of hair with amused wonder, assessing the anxiety flickering in those big blue eyes which bored into him like lasers. Kimberley was back. He grinned, stepping away to admire the slight figure in the understated beige shift, her skin freckled by the sun, her half-forgotten scent hitting him where it hurt most. He held her close.

"Poppet. Don't look so haunted," he murmured. "You're safe now. I'll get my lawyers to sort everything out."

"Oh, Raymond. I can't believe I'm home at last." Even to her ears, the words sounded trite but, for once, Kimberley Ada Carter spoke from the heart.

They settled back with the wine, glossing over the nightmare of the past weeks, trying, each in their own way, to turn back the clock. It seemed entirely natural that the rest of the afternoon would melt away in Raymond's splendid four-poster.

She unpacked her hand luggage and had a shower, fluffing up her hair which needed next to no attention. She gazed at herself in the full-length mirror angled at the end of the bed, ruefully admitting that Fernando's mama had been right. She was too thin. Her game of hide and seek had taken its toll. She sighed with pleasure, almost purring in the knowledge that she was back at last, safe, and that Raymond with all his powerful connections would sort everything out for her. She drained her glass, savouring the dry aftertaste of best bubbly.

They decided to eat out and he booked a table at one of the three-star eateries he normally used only for special clients. Glowing within the man's unlikely Saviour's nimbus, Kim finally admitted that being sheltered by an important figure like Turner was no bad thing. And Raymond, unlike the unlamented Fernando, was also man enough to allow her to stretch her wings. Even after a mere six hours Kimberley could see herself expanding in Raymond's shadow, taking her place on the board even, stepping into the top spot poor Andy had craved and for which he and two innocent women had paid such a terrible price.

They dawdled over brandy, Kim amusing him with her

mythical account of single life in Santiago. He didn't ask about her means of financing this mad excursion which was just as well as she was already wildly ad-libbing and the alcohol was making her perilously gabby.

"How about a romantic finale?" he whispered, cupping her hand in both his own as he leaned across the table. "Do you remember, sweetheart? That first time?"

"At the show flat?"

She giggled, recalling all too clearly the winter evening when the boss had appeared just as she and Andy were shutting up shop and had waved the rest of the staff off stage. 'We'll lock up,' he had insisted.

"Raymond, what a lovely idea! You brought the keys?"

"But of course."

"A new beginning, darling."

"Absolutely."

His driver, a sour-faced version of Rocco called Mackie, drove them across the river, eyeing the new-look Carter female in the rear-view mirror, well aware, as were all the Turner Development staff, of the runaround this office totty had survived with a boss not famous for his indulgence towards disloyal employees, let alone ex-lovers.

Turner House was mostly dark apart from the atrium, the upper floors largely unlet, only the illuminated elevator shafts pointing skywards like arrows. The doorman greeted them with a smart salute.

Raymond hugged his prize as they rose to the penthouse suite, her thin shoulders birdlike under his hand, her gait unsteady from the effects of too much champagne and a long long day on the road. She briefly reflected that life with Raymond Turner was no pushover: a full day's work for a full day's pay.

It was just as if she had never been away. The penthouse was cosier at night, the subdued lighting lending the over-designed interior a welcoming ambience, the scent of massed freesias on the coffee table subtly reassuring. The night was warm and the lights of the city gleamed across the river like a starry garland. Kimberley unlocked the patio doors with Raymond's keys and leaned on the balcony rail, watching the traffic on the river, feeling the breeze against her hot cheeks.

"I'll just check with the security team before we settle," he shouted from the hallway. "We don't want to set off any alarms." He touched some buttons which magically closed all but the patio blinds.

Kimberley nodded and lay on the sofa, drifting into a reverie as she heard the door quietly close behind him. Her lashes quivered, sheer exhaustion claiming her for what seemed only a few blissful minutes.

She awoke with a start, feeling the draught from the balcony chilling her bare arms. Glancing at her watch, she realised she had been sleeping for over two hours. Poor bloody Raymond. She swung her legs to the floor and half turned, then froze, her reflexes overstrung, instantly aware that the shadowy figure silhouetted in the doorway was not Raymond Turner. She stumbled to her feet, unsteady, the booze wreaking its havoc, then relaxed, recognising the man patiently waiting by the door.

"Oh Mackie, it's you. Phew! You gave me a fright for a minute. Did Raymond send you back for me? I conked out on the poor devil – too much wine and too little sleep." Her laugh bounced off the walls like a strangled cry, hardly a laugh at all. He nodded, saying nothing, and as she turned to gather up her bag and wrap he glided up behind her, soundless in his trainers.

She twisted round, suddenly afraid, realising with dismay that the hulk was still, on this warm summer night, wearing his driving gloves. He grabbed her arm, pinning her by the throat. Before she had a chance to cry out he lifted her off her feet without so much as a grunt. In seconds they were out on the balcony and her scream of terror as she plummeted to the ground whistled on the wind, blending with the night sounds of the river like the mournful hoot of a pleasure launch moving downstream.

Twenty-Nine

The flashing emergency lights in the forecourt of Turner House attracted little attention in the small hours of a Sunday morning. The suicide victim was not officially identified until Raymond Turner, the man, according to the guard at the Turner Development site office, who had brought the girl to the penthouse shortly after one o'clock in the morning, was tracked down at his club.

Dawn was breaking, the broken body decently obscured from the cold grey light by a blanket. The doctor had swiftly made his pronouncement, hardly a questionable verdict in view of the height from which the girl had thrown herself. Not even the time of death was in question, the crash witnessed by no less than three unfortunate passers-by and a taxi driver. Ackroyd had been called in as soon as the name Kimberley Carter came up on the screen, his irascible response aggravated by the knowledge that the one witness who could fill in the blanks in his Bailey investigation had topped herself.

"Any chance she was thrown off? Signs of a struggle in the flat?"

"No obvious indications. The place was locked, no break-in and all entrances strictly monitored."

A smell of river sludge drifted across the landscaped frontage of the luxurious tower block, its stench reminding Ackroyd of a blockage in the drains outside his own modest semi.

After the initial formalities the body was removed to the mortuary and Ackroyd arranged to interview Raymond Turner in his office later that day.

By eleven o'clock he had a rough idea of the timescale involved, the movements of the girl and the last man to see her alive nicely pigeonholed. The driver, Francis Mackie, confirmed he had driven the pair of them to the tower straight from the restaurant and the security men confirmed the time of their arrival and Turner's departure, the identity of the boss man and his former assistant all too familiar to the people on the gate. Ackroyd surveyed the jungle-like atrium, the area tastefully dotted about with flowing greenery.

"No other way up?"

"Only the service lift, sir, and that was locked up for the night."

"Fire exits?"

"Well," the man demurred, "if you're fit enough to run up twenty flights of stairs and down again without me or Ted noticing you might swing it." Ackroyd's jaundiced view of the unblinkered talents of security men left room for doubt. He jotted some notes in his book, pointing Lee towards the stairs to try it out with a stop watch. Well, why not? The lad was supposed to be fit, wasn't he?

Raymond Turner was alone in his office building apart from a caretaker on the gate, the empty rooms dusty in the summer sunshine slanting through roman blinds. He stood behind his desk as Ackroyd and his sergeant walked in, his complexion grey and unshaven, the double-breasted suit buttoned closely across his barrel chest as if the man felt an unseasonal chill in the air. He wore no tie, his neck rucked like an old sock.

They sat down, Lee taking out a small tape recorder to which Turner offered no objection.

"Shall we take it from the beginning, sir?"

Turner nodded, fumbling with a pen as he struggled to form a cohesive statement. The superintendent relaxed, recognising a decent witness for a change.

"As you may already be aware, Kimberley Carter lived with me for several months. Since October I think. She was also employed by the Development Corporation as a design consultant."

"A good worker?"

"Excellent. A real flair. I also trusted her with personal work which made her disloyalty a double blow. Of course, as she is – was – much younger than I, I suppose the break-up was only to be expected. She fell in love with Bailey, poor girl, and expected to run away with him so she believed. Utterly deceived by the man's plausibility, as were we all, sadly."

"You were angry?"

"Initially furious. My vanity is such that I had not seen the danger signals until it was too late. I employed a man to follow her, I'm ashamed to admit, but such moves are useless, merely fanning the hope that one was being too suspicious. One gets more vulnerable in middle-age, don't you agree, Superintendent? A doting old fool," he added with asperity.

"She disappeared without a word?"

"I heard nothing from her for weeks. Until about a month ago when she telephoned me from Chile. She'd been living in Santiago, trying to come to terms with the shock of learning about Bailey's homicidal spree."

"She had no warning of his sadistic tendencies?"

"Only intuition, she said. I didn't press her – it was not a subject either of us wished to dwell upon. After some weeks of consideration I agreed to take her back and Kimberley arrived home yesterday."

"In good spirits?"

"Delighted to be in England again. Chile had been a bad experience I gather. Kimberley was a Londoner through and through. Homesick. It was only when Bailey was under lock and key she felt it was safe to return."

Ackroyd tried to interrupt but let it go, the man's narrative taking on a rhythm he was loath to break.

"As I was saying, she arrived back in the afternoon after a trying journey. I should have made some allowances for her fatigue, Superintendent, but love is blind. It was wonderful to have her back. We dined late and things seemed to be moving along smoothly."

"Why did you go to the penthouse?"

Turner laughed, dragging thick fingers through his hair, abashed by the question.

"To be honest it was a silly romantic gesture. I wanted to go back to the beginning, to start over. Can you understand? We first made love at the show flat, an impulsive coupling and a tender memory for me. I hoped that by going back there we could recapture the old emotion, and let's face it, Superintendent, I do own the building."

"Yes, of course. Please go on."

"Kimberley had been drinking all afternoon and we rather pushed the boat out at La Fontaine."

"The restaurant in Beauchamp Place?"

"Quite so. My man drove us to the House about one o'clock but once we were settled Kimberley turned nasty, accusing me of sexual harassment – as an employee you realise! –

215

threatening legal proceedings. All utter rubbish, of course. It was the drink talking. Kimberley never had a head for alcohol. She was tired, of course. I should have been less amorous, curbed my natural demands. Then, believe it or not, she attacked me. A vicious little cat when roused. I decided to call it a day. I picked up the keys and left her to cool off. Something of a prickteaser that girl."

Lee stifled a guffaw and coughed, Ackroyd throwing a warning shot across his bows which fortunately went unnoticed by the ravaged tycoon pouring out his all too familiar tale of woe.

"I left her to sober up and got Mackie to drive me to a gaming club, then sent him home. I was in a mood to make a night of it, take out my temper on the tables. A private club. I am a member, of course, you can check my arrival, they all know me well. I regret Lady Luck was not on my side last night and I lost more than any sensible man should have to admit to. Having dismissed my driver and with no inclination to go home alone I took a room and retired well after four o'clock."

"We shall, I must warn you, check all this at your club. And we shall confirm your statement with Mr Mackie. A reliable employee, someone of long standing, sir?"

"Ex-army. A fine family man of exemplary character. A wife and kids. Mrs Mackie will naturally vouch for my driver getting home before two, an early Saturday night for the poor devil. A chauffeur's life's no bed of roses."

Ackroyd signalled Lee to pack up and rose to go.

"One thing I must ask, Superintendent. Did that poor girl suffer? I shall never forgive myself for abandoning her like that, in the drunken state she was in. It was obviously an accident, falling off the balcony, disorientated presumably.

I must arrange for all the balconies to be fitted with safety bars . . ."

"The lady died instantly. Just after three o'clock. A fall like that . . ." Ackroyd shrugged, unwilling to recall the mess of blood and bones he had been obliged to examine. The two policemen trooped out, travelling back to the mortuary without exchanging a word, the ghastly business all too fresh in their minds. The man was kidding himself. Disorientated? She would have had to climb up to fall, a skinny tart like that. An accident? No way. Even so, Ackroyd made a note to question the pathologist about drugs. Maybe the silly kid was having a bad trip, alcohol being the least of her worries.

Culley felt gutted when he found out he'd missed out on the final act of the Griffith drama. Kimberley a suicide? Not the girl he remembered. Whatever had happened after Venice to drive her to dive off a skyscraper? A scrap with Turner? Hardly. Not unless Kim thought she had blown her last chance . . .

But Ackroyd was adamant. Absolutely no evidence of foul play and Turner, the last man to see her alive, pinpointed at every stage of that summer night. Even so, as Tom languidly explained to Marianne as they stuffed popcorn in the back row of the Minema, Kimberley Carter dead was very convenient for both the men in her life, her evidence the only proof of Raymond Turner's dodgy dealing and her absence leaving a black hole in the case against bloody Bailey.

Win some, lose some, as they say.